[redacted]

PLURCH ACADEMY

FOR DISRUPTIVE BOYS

curse of the
bizarro
beetle

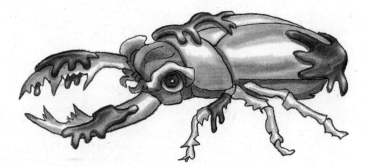

GROSSET & DUNLAP
Published by the Penguin Group
Penguin Group (USA) Inc., 375 Hudson Street,
New York, New York 10014, USA
Penguin Group (Canada), 90 Eglinton Avenue East, Suite 700,
Toronto, Ontario M4P 2Y3, Canada
(a division of Pearson Penguin Canada Inc.)
Penguin Books Ltd., 80 Strand, London WC2R 0RL, England
Penguin Group Ireland, 25 St. Stephen's Green, Dublin 2, Ireland
(a division of Penguin Books Ltd.)
Penguin Group (Australia), 250 Camberwell Road, Camberwell,
Victoria 3124, Australia
(a division of Pearson Australia Group Pty. Ltd.)
Penguin Books India Pvt. Ltd., 11 Community Centre,
Panchsheel Park, New Delhi—110 017, India
Penguin Group (NZ), 67 Apollo Drive, Rosedale,
North Shore 0632, New Zealand
(a division of Pearson New Zealand Ltd.)
Penguin Books (South Africa) (Pty.) Ltd., 24 Sturdee Avenue,
Rosebank, Johannesburg 2196, South Africa

Penguin Books Ltd., Registered Offices:
80 Strand, London WC2R 0RL, England

Copyright © 2010 Julie Berry and Sally Gardner. All rights reserved.
Published by Grosset & Dunlap, a division of Penguin Young Readers
Group, 345 Hudson Street, New York, New York 10014.
GROSSET & DUNLAP is a trademark of Penguin Group (USA) Inc.
Printed in the U.S.A.

Typeset in Imprint.

Library of Congress Cataloging-in-Publication Data is available.

ISBN 978-0-448-45360-6   10 9 8 7 6 5 4 3 2 1

SPLURCH ACADEMY
FOR DISRUPTIVE BOYS

curse of the
bizarro
beetle

by Julie Gardner Berry and Sally Faye Gardner

Grosset & Dunlap
An Imprint of Penguin Group (USA) Inc.

To my sons, Joseph, Daniel, Adam,
and David.
—J.G.B.

To my nieces, Elspeth, Claire, Sophie,
and Liney.
—S.F.G.

A Word of Warning
to All Disruptive Boys

You wouldn't believe me if I told you about Splurch Academy for Disruptive Boys, a forgotten boarding school far away from anywhere. Rats fill the cellars. Cockroaches climb the walls. Slime and cobwebs cover just about everything else.

Those are the least of its problems.

That's where they send boys *like you* to live, night and day, when they've been too naughty for too long, and their parents and schoolteachers decide they can't take it anymore. They farm them out to Splurch Academy for Disruptive Boys, run by headmaster Dr. Archibald Farley, educator, scientist, inventor, psychopath. He promises he'll fix bad boys forever.

He takes them away to his school.

They hardly ever come back.

I'll bet you don't believe there is such a place.

Neither did Cody Mack.

I'll bet you don't think your parents would go that far.

Neither did Cody Mack.

You'd better watch yourself.

Cody's parents hoped drastic steps could save their son from a life of crime, so they sent Cody to Splurch. It didn't take long to learn what a prison it was. The kids dressed in uniforms and ate toxic gruel. They were sent to dungeons for minor crimes. They were forced to write *essays*. And they weren't allowed to leave the building.

Especially at night.

Leaving the Splurch Academy building at night is *extremely* unwise.

When the moon rises and the sun sets,
the teachers go outside and transform.

Into vampires.

Werewolves.

Frankensteins.

Monsters of every shape and description
that want nothing more than children for a
midnight snack.

And these are monsters with a plan. Just
weeks ago, Dr. Farley and his hench-teachers
unleashed a sinister plot to swap the boys'
brains with the brains of trained rats.

Farley's ego was his downfall. He got cocky. He
got careless. He invited his mother, Madame
Desdemona Sackville-Smack, the Grand
Inquisitrix of the League of Reform Schools,
to come see how well the "boys" were doing.
He invited parents, too. Farley was sure they'd
all be dazzled by the boys' fake progress.

He overlooked one thing.

Cody Mack.

Cody and his friends, Carlos, Sully, Ratface, Mugsy, and Victor, all inside their rat bodies, sabotaged the show and swapped everyone's brains back using Farley's evil machine, the Rebellio-Rodent Recipronator. The party fell to pieces. The parents flipped out. Farley's mom had to hypnotize the parents to erase their memories. Farley was so furious with Cody, he crossed the threshold of Splurch Academy and tried to eat him.

Which is a big no-no. Farley's mom got mad.

You don't want to make Desdemona Sackville-Smack mad.

She sent Farley to time-out in a crypt deep underground, below the school.

At least, down there, he can't torture the boys anymore.

Or so she thinks.

But you should never, ever underestimate Dr. Archibald Farley.

Don't say I didn't warn you.

Grade Five

Possibly the most disruptive bunch of boys Splurch Academy has ever seen.

Cody Mack, age 11

The Master of Disruption. The Sultan of Schemes. The Prince of Plots. The Demigod of Dastardly Deeds. A pint-size Lord of Chaos. The ringleader of the fifth-grade band of brothers, and every teacher's worst nightmare.

Carlos Ferrari, age 10

Cody Mack's best friend. Give him a rubber band, a paper clip, and a can of shaving cream, and he'll turn them into a weapon of mass *disruption*. It's not his fault things tend to blow up when he's around.

Mugsy, aka Percival Porsein, age 11

This kid will eat *anything* as long as it has ketchup on it. Don't tease him about his teddy bear or he'll sit on you. He has a habit of accidentally breaking things, like other people's ribs, but really, he means well.

Ratface, aka Rufus Larsen, age 10

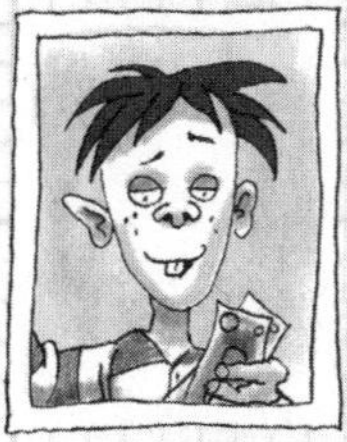

The one kid at Splurch Academy who felt perfectly at home in a rat's body. He's whiny; he's annoying; he has weird ideas. Nothing is safe from this light-fingered little thief.

Sully, aka Sullivan Sanders, age 10

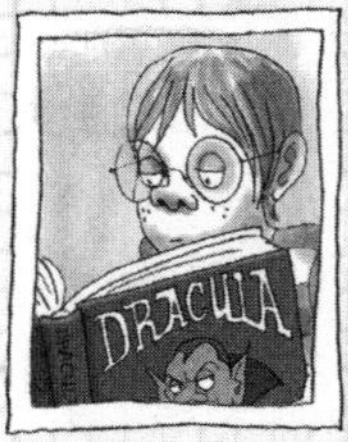
DRACULA

Brave as an earthworm. Athletic as cooked spaghetti. Minus his glasses he's as blind as a mole. Still, being a genius has its advantages. This bookworm won't speak to adults. Period.

Victor Schmitz, age 11

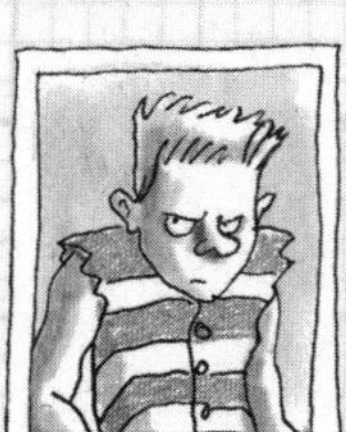

Anger issues got him sent to Splurch, and nothing's changed so far. A good pick for a tug-of-war team, but you don't want to challenge him to an arm-wrestling match. If you do, it's safer if *you* lose.

The Teachers

Dr. Archibald Farley, Headmaster

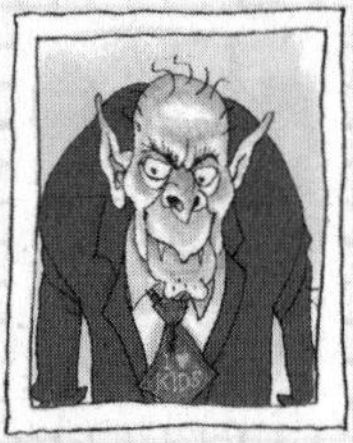
KIDS

The egotistical mastermind behind the torture of innocent disruptive boys. With his vampire strength and his mad science cunning, this evil headmaster is never without a plan to make Cody and his friends suffer.

Nurse Bilgewater

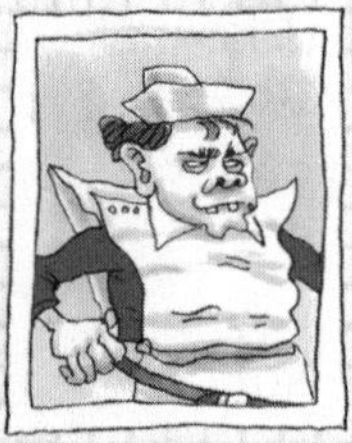

Strong as an ox and as kind-hearted as a feeding shark, Beulah Bilgewater is Splurch Academy's medical specialist. Whatever you do, don't get sick. Once this evil nurse gets her tentacles on you, there's no escape.

Mr. Fronk

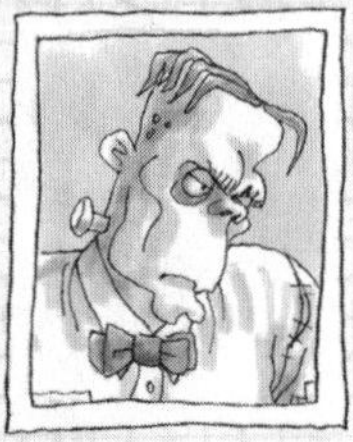

A lumbering carcass of a fifth-grade teacher who sleeps like a corpse through every class. His two fears: fire and boys who prefer comic books.

Griselda, the Cafeteria Lady

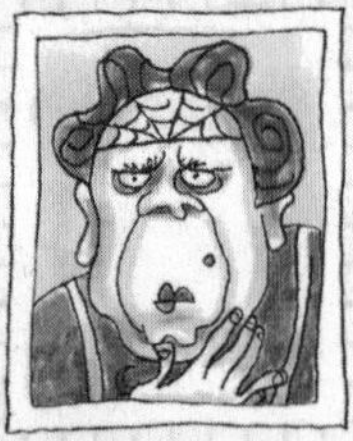

The only thing worse than her cooking is her complaining about her aches and pains. Wait. Never mind. Her cooking's worse.

Mr. Howell

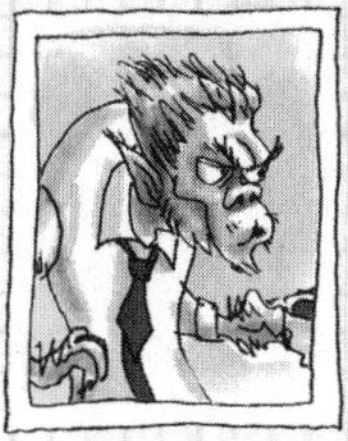

Go ahead. Try to run away from Splurch Academy. This mangy fleabag will even give you a head start. He sprints like a wolf and gnaws on bones for lunch. Better steer clear when the moon comes out . . .

Ivanov, the Hall Monitor

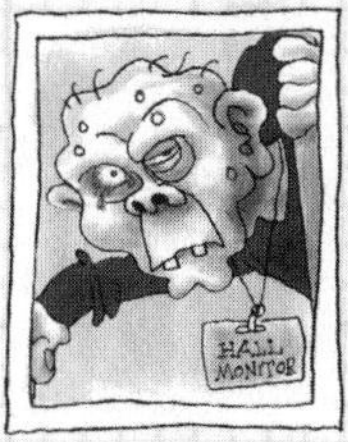
HALL
MONITOR

This jack-of-all-trades does the dirty work of keeping the Academy clean. Sort of. He'd rather do the dirty work of tattling on kids.

Librarian

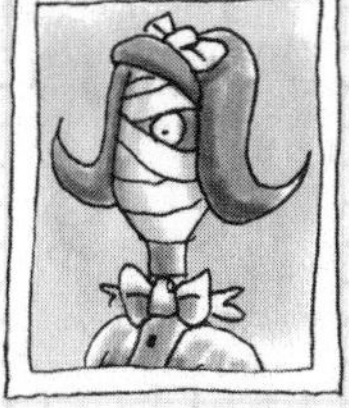

Does she have a name? Does she ever speak? Whose side is she on? No one is sure. But don't raise your voice in her library. Not if you want to own your own tongue.

Miss Threadbare

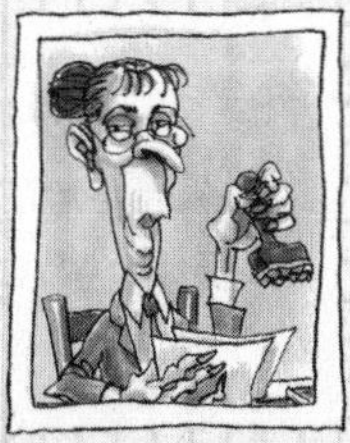

This bony, spindly, scraggly bag o' knuckles and teeth is Headmaster Farley's secretary by day—a bat-winged hawk-monster by night. Don't be slow when *she* tells you to stand for the pledge.

CHAPTER ONE

THE COFFIN

A crescent moon hung low over the topmost towers of Splurch Academy. Across the windswept grounds, wolves howled and night birds moaned.

Inside the school, all was dark. Dozens of boys slept uncomfortably on ancient mattresses in the gloomy dormitories, dreaming of ice cream and swimming pools and life the way it used to be, long ago, before they were sent to this nightmare school.

Cody Mack was one of them. But he wasn't alone.

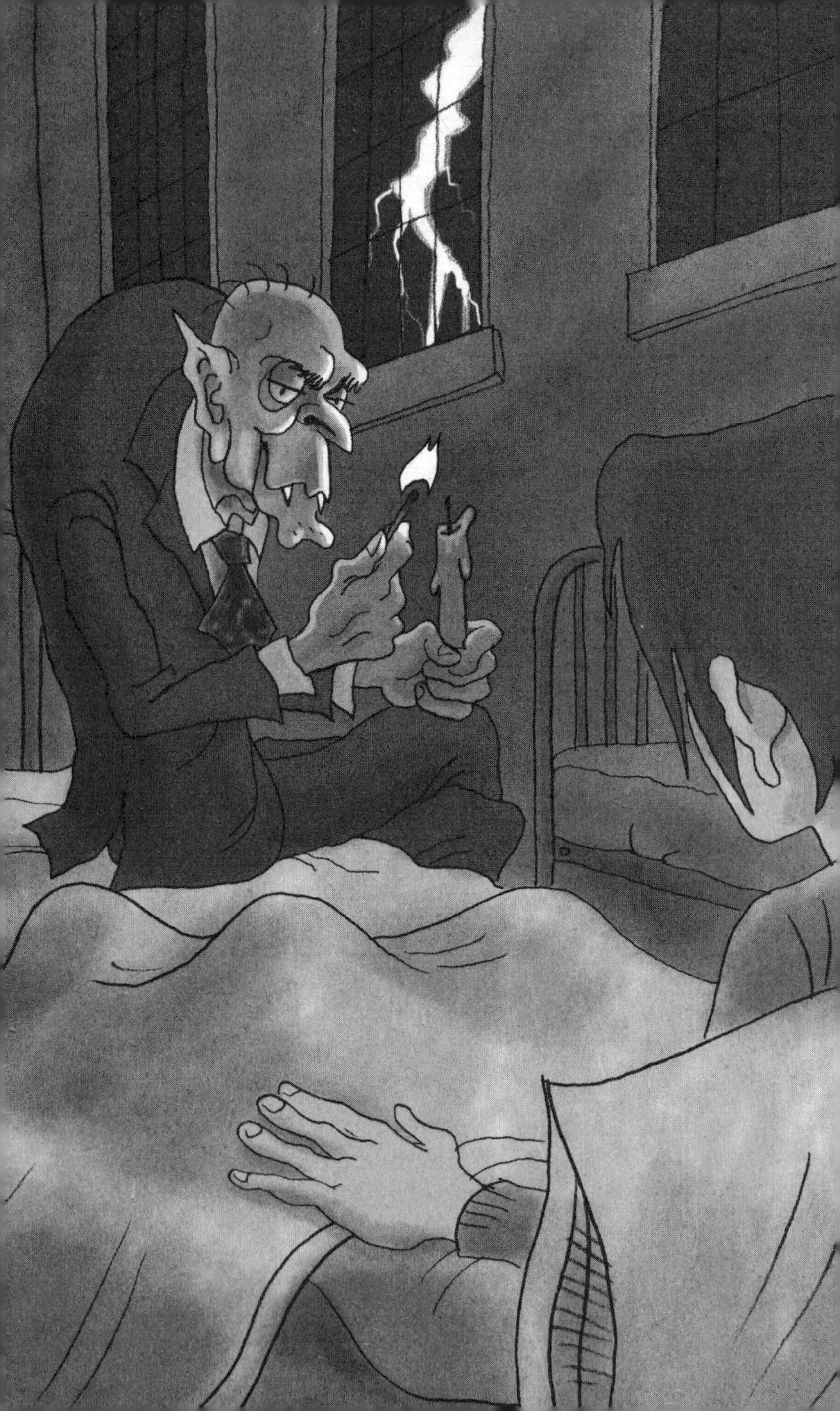

Someone tapped his shoulder.

Cody sat up in his bunk, rubbing his eyes. He couldn't see anybody in the dark room. But someone, he knew, was there.

A flash of lightning lit the room.

It was Headmaster Archibald Farley, the psychotic vampire who ran this evil school.

He lit a candle and gestured for Cody to follow him. They walked slowly down a long, dim corridor to an ancient elevator. Cody wanted to resist, to fight, to turn and run away from his sworn enemy, but some unseen force prevented him. He had to do what Farley said.

They got into the elevator, and it began to descend. Second floor. First floor. Dungeon. But the elevator kept plunging down, down, down, growing faster by the second.

The elevator stopped with a clang and opened into a room lit only by a flickering torch. Inside the room were several long boxes. Coffins! Cody lifted their lids and found them full of dirt and old bones. He shuddered. Farley pointed to another coffin, and, reluctantly, Cody threw back the lid.

3

Inside the coffin lay . . . Dr. Farley!

Cody blinked and took a step back. There were two of them! The one who brought him here, and the one inside the coffin, whose eyes were closed in sleep and whose teeth gleamed in the candlelight. Clutched in his long fingers was a strange device that Cody knew only too well—the Rebellio-Rodent Recipronator, Farley's evil brain-swapping invention.

"But we broke the Recipronator!" Cody yelled. "We smashed it to smithereens!"

And that was true. But here was Farley—

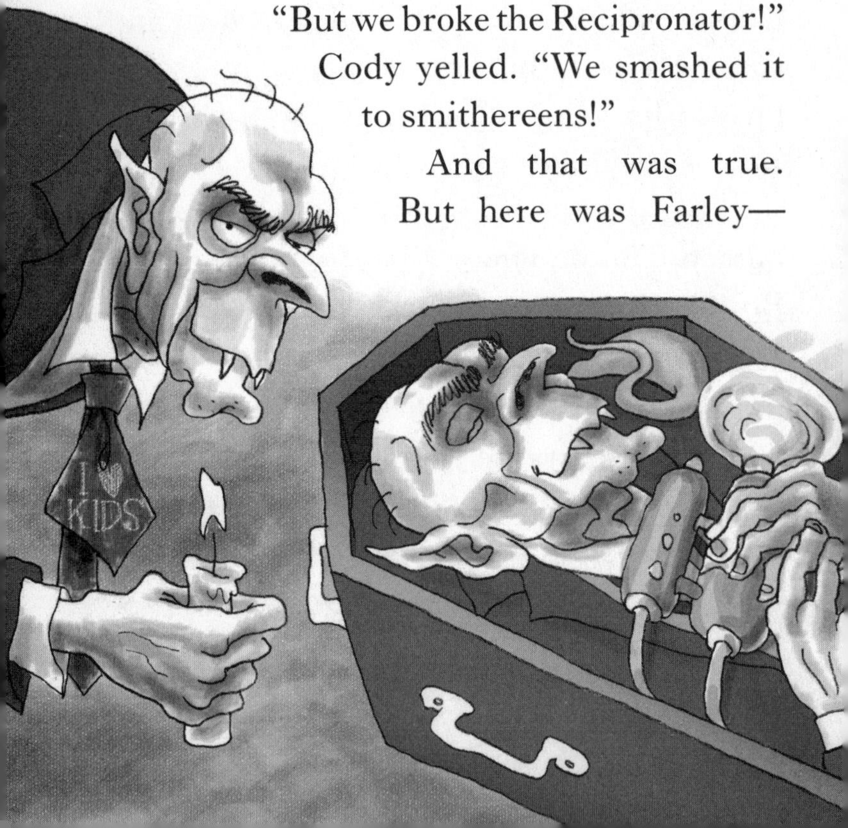
I ♥ KIDS

two Farleys, in fact—and a perfectly whole Recipronator. *Not good.*

Something moved near the sleeping Farley's shoulder. It was Rasputin, Farley's old pet rat, nibbling on a huge chunk of cheese. He scampered over to Cody and handed him the cheese.

"Thanks, Rasputin, old pal," Cody said, and he took a big bite of the cheese. *Dee-licious.*

The Farley in the coffin opened his eyes and sat up. Both Farleys leered at Cody. They seized him and then pinned the Recipronator suction nozzle against Cody's ear, attaching the other nozzle to Coffin Farley's ear. A third nozzle appeared on the Recipronator, attached to a helmet on Rasputin's little rat head. *Wait, there's not supposed to be three of them*, Cody thought. They were going to suck his brain out one more time! Only instead of swapping him with a rat, they were going to swap him with . . . Farley? *And* Rasputin?

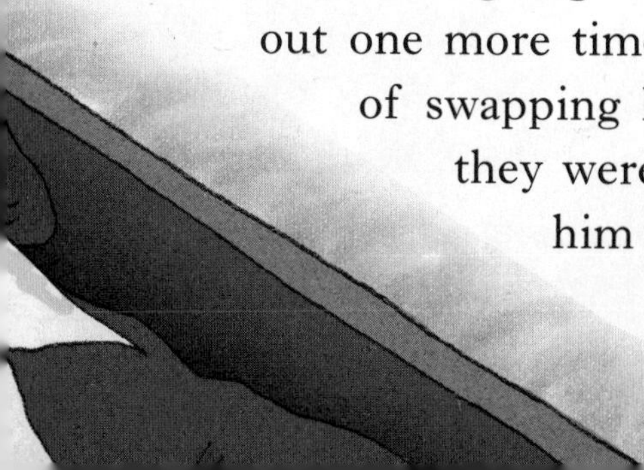

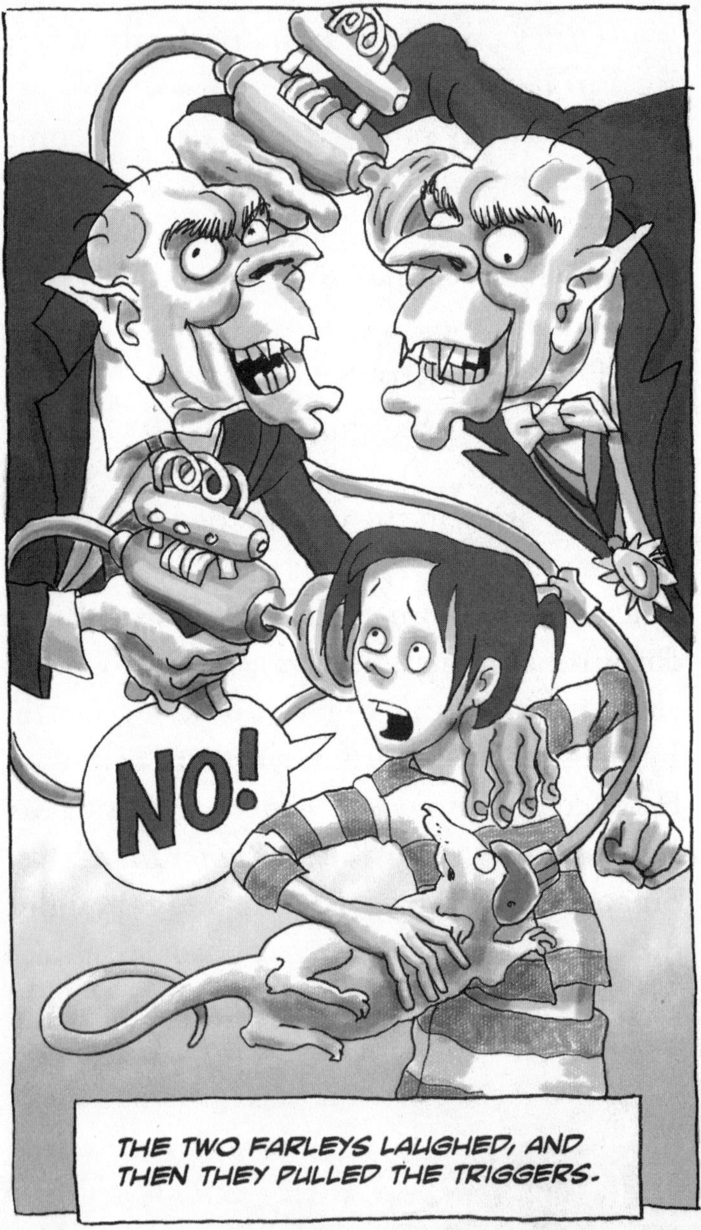
NO!
THE TWO FARLEYS LAUGHED, AND THEN THEY PULLED THE TRIGGERS.

CHAPTER TWO

THE RAID

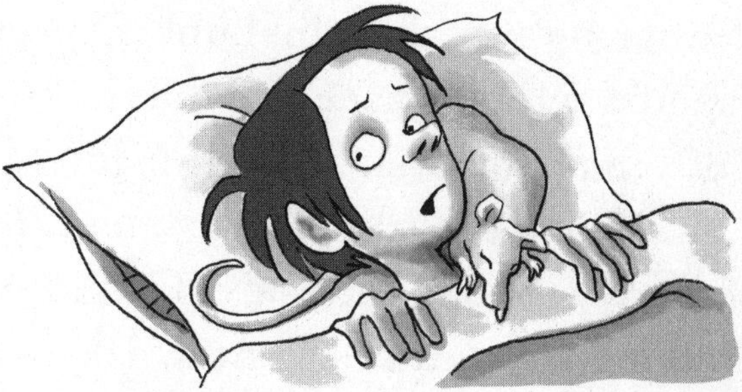

Cody's eyes opened. It was dark. Pitch-dark. No torch, no candle.

And no Farley.

It was only a dream. Of course it was! He'd watched with his own eyes, weeks ago, when Madame Desdemona Sackville-Smack banished Farley to a crypt deep under the school. The ground had opened up like an earthquake! There was no way Cody could get down there.

Then the dream faded from his mind. Rasputin, Farley's old pet rat who once had Cody's brain in his skull, lay curled up on his pillow, soft and warm and comforting. He'd been hanging around Cody ever since Farley was banished. Cody figured the rat felt closer to him than anyone else, since they'd once shared each other's brains. It was kind of nice having a pet share his bunk. Especially in a spooky, creepy place like this.

Cody had forgiven Rasputin for biting him on the hand back on that fateful night when Farley tried to eat Cody. That bite was sure taking a long time to heal. It was still sore, but Cody was used to that by now. He closed his eyes and went back to sleep.

The next morning, before the breakfast bell rang, Cody and his disruptive classmates tiptoed down the dark stairs leading to the cafeteria. Ratface, the master thief (diagnosis: totally obnoxious) led the way, while Sully, the brainiac (refuses to speak to adults), Cody's closest friend, Carlos, the inventor (blows things up), Victor, tough athlete (anger management issues), and Mugsy (zero motivation) followed.

"Are you sure this will work?" Mugsy said. He was practically drooling. "There better be good eats."

"Trust me," Ratface said. "The pantry's loaded."

"If it isn't," Victor grumbled, "I'll bust your head."

"If the teachers catch us stealing," Sully whimpered, "they'll use our heads for bowling balls."

"This isn't stealing," Mugsy said. "It's survival. The school is *supposed* to feed us. Real food, not cockroach raisin bran."

"So, Cody," Carlos said, "what're you gonna be for Halloween?"

Sully butted in. "Halloween doesn't happen at Splurch Academy, Carlos. Not for kids."

"Yeah, but *if* it did," Carlos said, "what would you dress up as?"

"A kid stuck in a prison school, I guess," Cody said. "I've already got the costume."

"I'm serious!" Carlos said. His eyes got a sad, faraway look. "Last year, I was Lord Galactitron."

Ratface got excited. "I was a brain-sucking alien zombie. I had a plunger sticking out of my mouth."

"My granny made my costume," Mugsy said. "I was a super-size order of fries. I squirted myself all over with real ketchup."

"Gross!" Ratface said.

"Yeah, Granny wasn't happy about that."

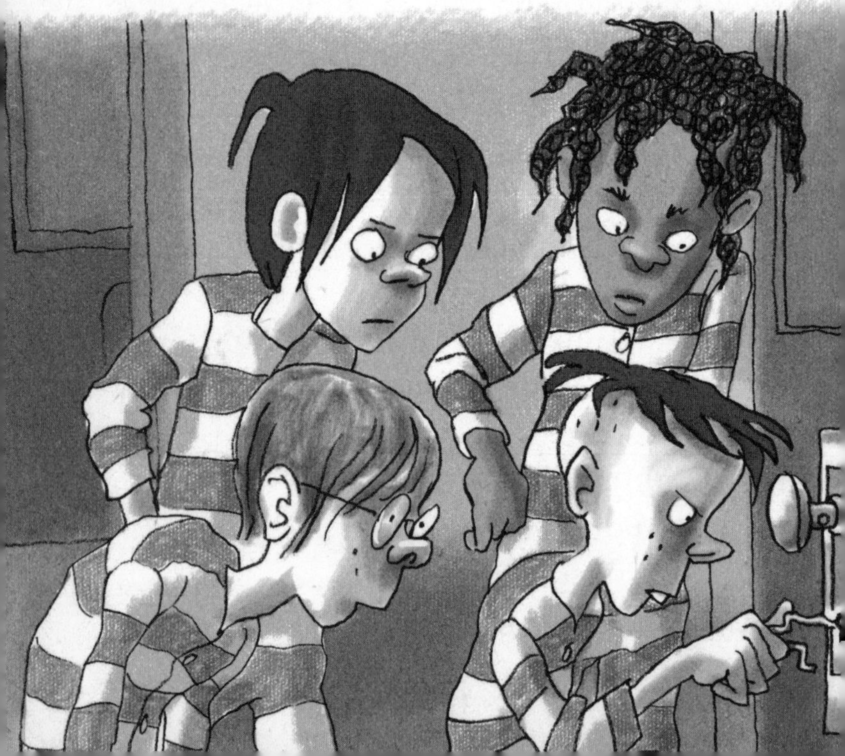

They reached the kitchen door. Ratface twisted the doorknob, listened, then stuck an unbent paperclip into the lock and listened some more. There was a click, and the door swung open.

"Bingo," he said. "We're in. Come on!"

They closed the door to the kitchen.

"Welcome to the best thing about this lousy school," Ratface said. "Griselda's pantry. Feast your eyes."

He threw open the door to a long, skinny room full of shelves.

Their eyes gradually adjusted to the dim light. On one wall, the shelves were stocked with dusty, cobwebby cans and bottles labeled INSTA-GRUEL and FORTIFIED BEET STEW and DEHYDRATED CABBAGE NUGGETS. But on the other wall were . . .

"Doughnuts!" Carlos whimpered.

"Not just doughnuts," Cody said as he ripped into a box. "*Store-bought* Doopy Powdered Doughnuts!"

"Lookit all these bottles of ketchup!" Mugsy said, jumping up to reach a higher shelf. "Aren't they beautiful?"

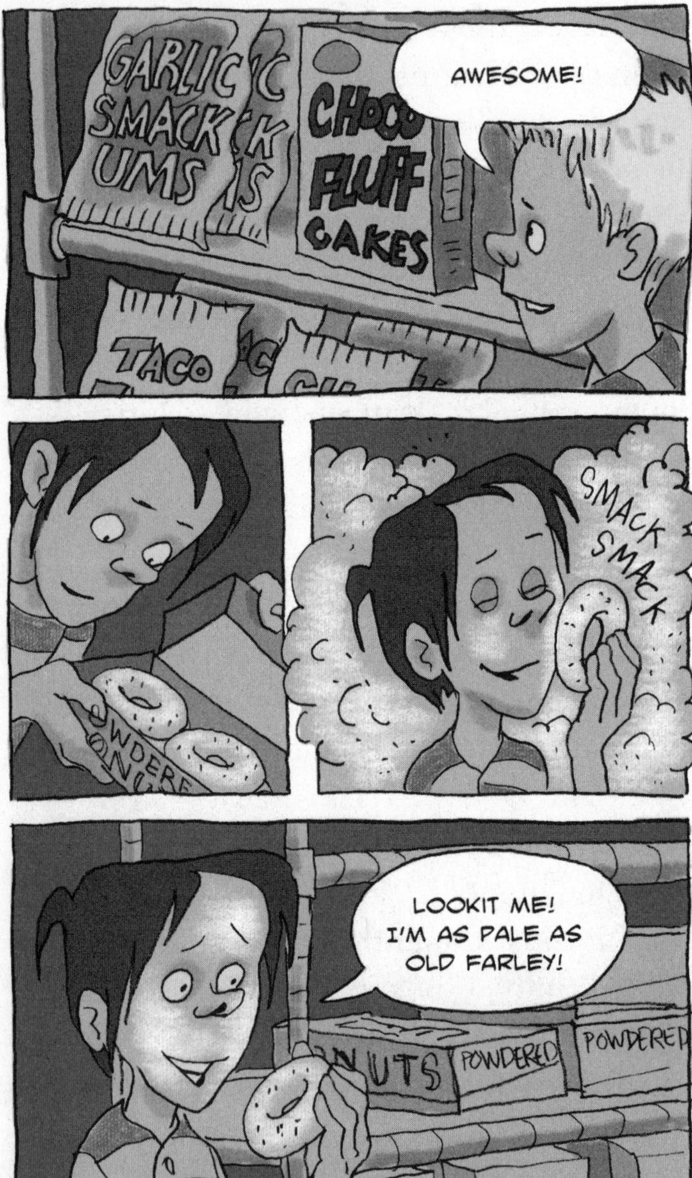
GARLIC SMACK UMS
CHOCO FLUFF CAKES
TACO
AWESOME!
SMACK SMACK
LOOKIT ME! I'M AS PALE AS OLD FARLEY!
POWDERED
POWDERED

"Maybe that's who you should be for Halloween," Carlos said.

Cody shuddered. "No, thanks."

Victor smacked his face with his doughnut. "I'm the Splurch Academy ghost!"

Mugsy smacked his face with his doughnut. "I'm a marshmallow pie!"

Ratface smacked his face with his doughnut. "I'm a pair of tighty-whities!"

Sully took a bite of his doughnut. "One of your *new* pairs, you mean."

Click.

"What was that?" Ratface whispered. "Everybody, hide!"

They ducked under the lowest pantry shelves.

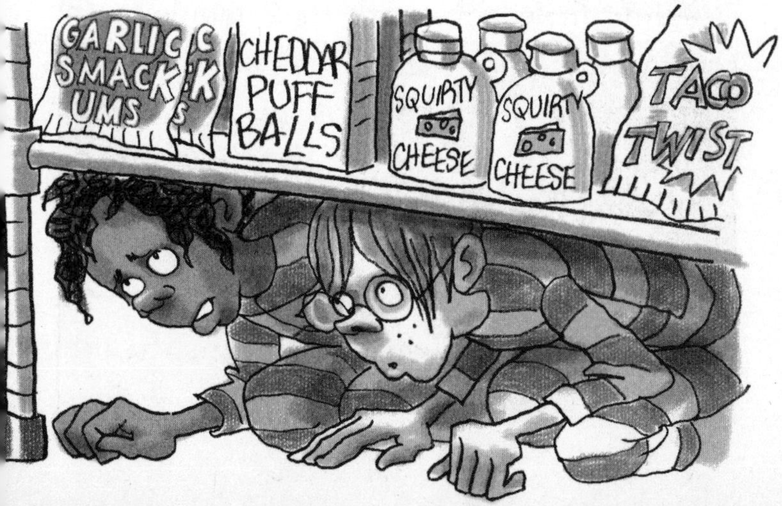
GARLIC SMACK UMS
CHEDDAR PUFF BALLS
SQUIRTY CHEESE
SQUIRTY CHEESE
TACO TWIST

"Only a moron wouldn't see us here," Carlos whispered. They waited, cringing, trying to make themselves as small and invisible as possible.

There's almost nothing worse than waiting to get caught, Cody thought.

The lights clicked on in the kitchen. From where he crouched, Cody could see white shoes and thick, scaly ankles. It was Nurse Bilgewater, acting Headmistress. Next to Farley, she was the creepiest grown-up at Splurch Academy. She was a nurse, but she wasn't interested in *relieving* suffering. She liked to *inflict* it.

"I smell thieves!" she cackled as she passed by the pantry door. "Grubby, filthy, stealing little boys with their hands in the cookie jar!"

"Cookie jar?" Mugsy whispered. "I didn't see any . . ."

"Can it or they'll find us!" Victor hissed.

The footsteps stopped in front of the door. Nurse Bilgewater wrenched the pantry door open.

14

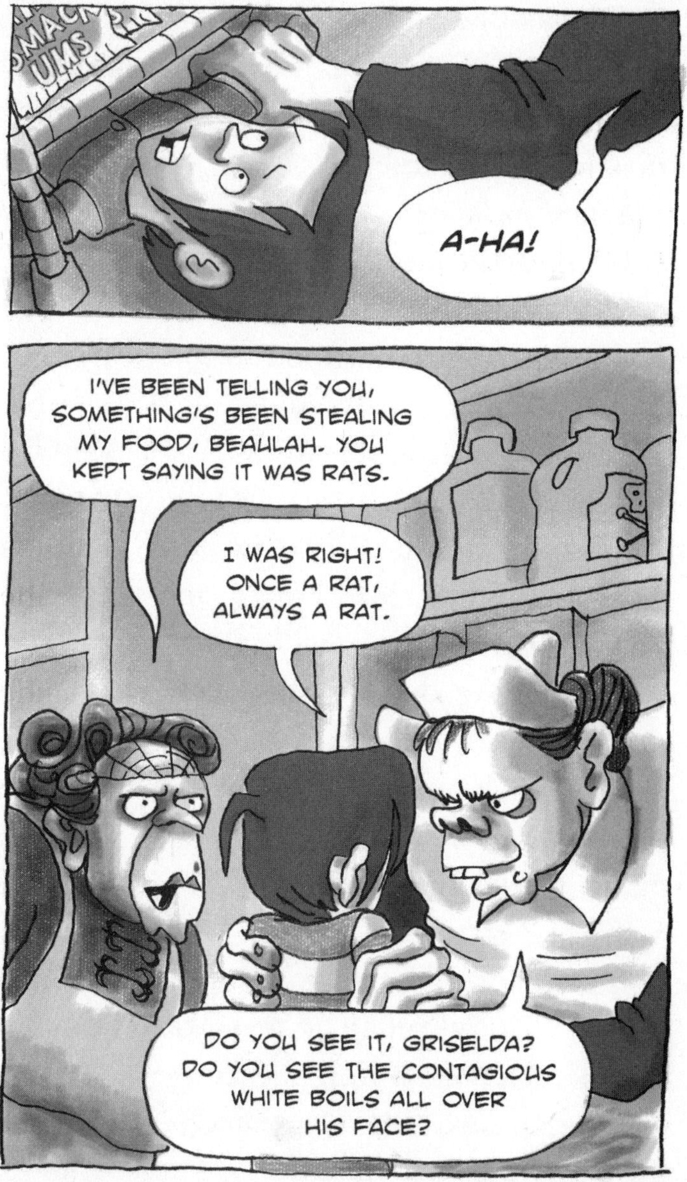
A-HA!
I'VE BEEN TELLING YOU, SOMETHING'S BEEN STEALING MY FOOD, BEAULAH. YOU KEPT SAYING IT WAS RATS.
I WAS RIGHT! ONCE A RAT, ALWAYS A RAT.
DO YOU SEE IT, GRISELDA? DO YOU SEE THE CONTAGIOUS WHITE BOILS ALL OVER HIS FACE?

"Looks like powdered sug—"

"Just as I feared," Nurse Bilgewater said, peering at the boys cringing under the shelves. "These boys have a bad case of splagged gaskers."

Griselda gasped. "Is it catching?"

"Very," Nurse Bilgewater said. "They'll all need to be quarantined in the infirmary. Immediately."

Griselda wrung her hands. "You mean I'll have to *bring* them their food? On trays?"

"Don't overdo it, Grizzy," Nurse Bilgewater said. "Weak broth should do the trick. Bring them a bowl every other day."

"For how long?" the cafeteria lady persisted.

Nurse Bilgewater's big, fishy eyes gleamed as they goggled at Cody. "No less than a week. Possibly eight."

Cody struggled against Bilgewater's iron grip. "You can't lock us away for eight weeks!" Cody yelled. "You great, big, fat tub of rotten calamari!"

They heard another voice. "What's all the commotion in here?"

The other boys shuddered as two of Splurch Academy's most loathsome monster teachers appeared—Mr. Fronk, the Frankenmonster, and Mr. Howell, the werewolf. Mr. Howell sniffed at Cody's armpits like an overgrown dog.

"Morning, gentlemen," Bilgewater said. "Found these sickly boys out and about, contaminating the food supply with their germs. They're going to need to spend several weeks locked away in quarantine." A slow smile spread over her fat, fishy

SNIFF
SNIFF

lips. "Where I can take extra good care of them."

"And look who the ringleader is," Mr. Fronk observed. "No surprise there. Cody Mack."

Mr. Howell chuckled. "Weeks? Why, they'll miss Halloween, won't they?"

"What a pity." Mr. Fronk's deep voice sounded like a school bus engine downshifting. "They'll be locked away in the sick ward while we . . . er . . . ahem. While we get on with our usual business."

Miss Threadbare, the school secretary, poked her long, beaklike nose through the pantry door.

"Congratulations, Beulah," she said, patting Nurse Bilgewater on the shoulder. "Not even Farley could have thought up such a perfect solution to our little childcare problem."

Nurse Bilgewater batted her eyelashes. "I am rather a genius, aren't I?"

CHAPTER THREE

THE INFIRMARY

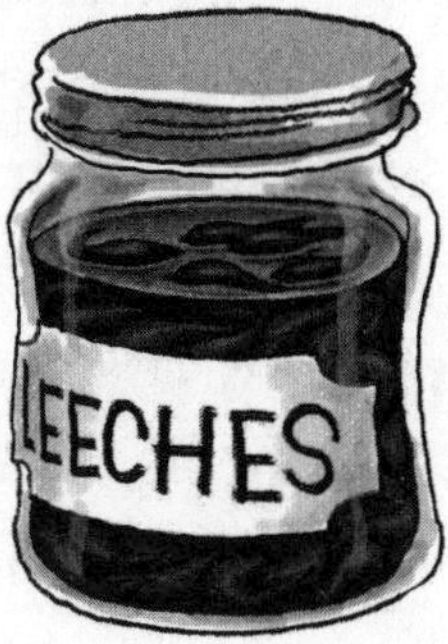
LEECHES

The cots in the infirmary looked like they'd been used by wounded soldiers in the Civil War. Cobwebs dangled in sheets from the ceiling, obscuring the tall windows, while rows of medical instruments hung from pegs along one wall. Jars of blue antiseptic held smaller instruments, while other jars held squishy things that might have been body parts. The only sort of modern thing in the room was a refrigerator.

"See you later, Bilgewater," Mr. Howell said. "We'll leave you to your fun."

"Righty-o," Nurse Bilgewater replied.

She rubbed her hands together. "Let's see. Where shall we begin? How about a nice dose of medicine to make 'em puke all morning. That'd be fun to watch."

Cody and his friends exchanged nervous looks. Ratface's cheeks bulged like he was already puking at the thought.

"Then again . . . I'd have to clean it up. How about operations? It's been so long . . . I don't have any anesthesia, but who cares?"

Sully crashed to the floor in a dead faint. Nurse Bilgewater ignored him. Cody slapped his cheeks and woke him up.

Nurse Bilgewater snapped her fingers. "I know!" She took a huge, evil-looking device off the pegs on the wall and plugged its power cord into an outlet. "Nothing better for splagged gaskers than a little electroshock therapy." She advanced toward them, the tip of her cattle prod sizzling.

"Um, Cody," Mugsy whispered. His skin was the color of moldy cheese. "Wh-wh-what do we do now?"

"On the count of three," Cody whispered. "Oh, never mind. RUN!"

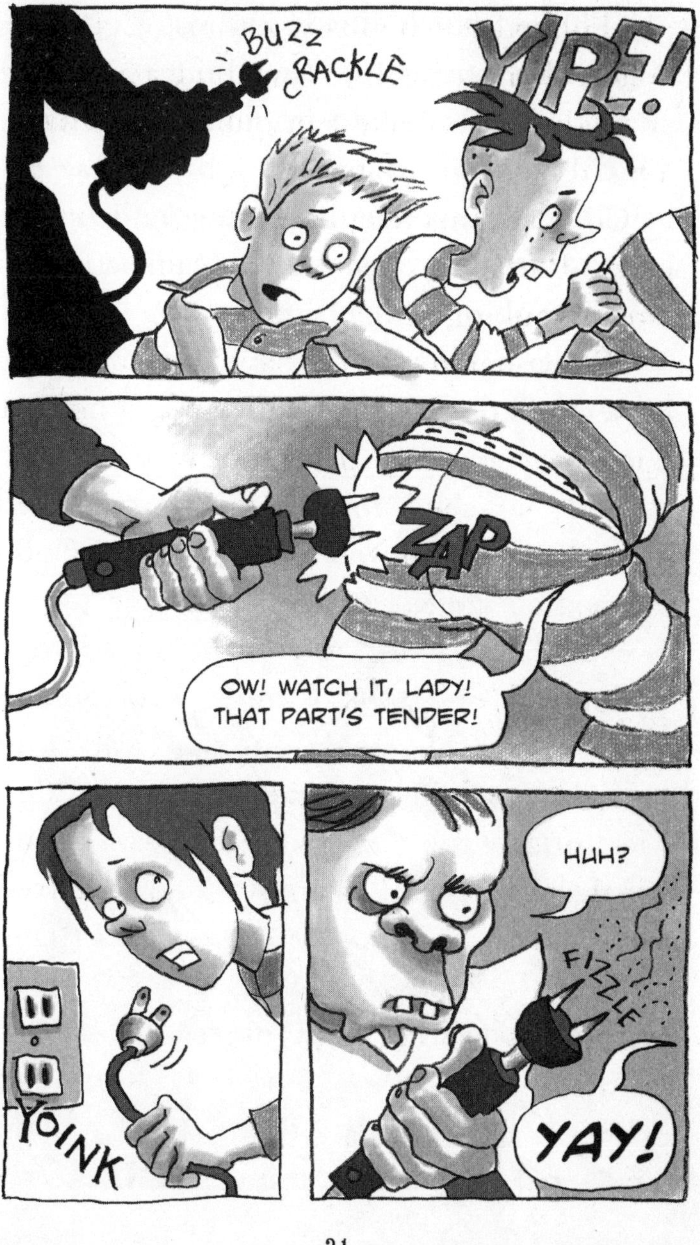
BUZZ
CRACKLE
YIPE!
ZAP
OW! WATCH IT, LADY! THAT PART'S TENDER!
YOINK
HUH?
FIZZLE
YAY!

"Think you're clever, do you?" Nurse Bilgewater said. "If you aren't ready for therapy, then it's old-fashioned medicine you need." She reached for a brown jug on a shelf and dunked a huge squeeze dropper into the mouth of the jug. Up came a thick, viscous glob of brown slime.

"Codfish liver oil cures most ailments, Cody Mack," she said.

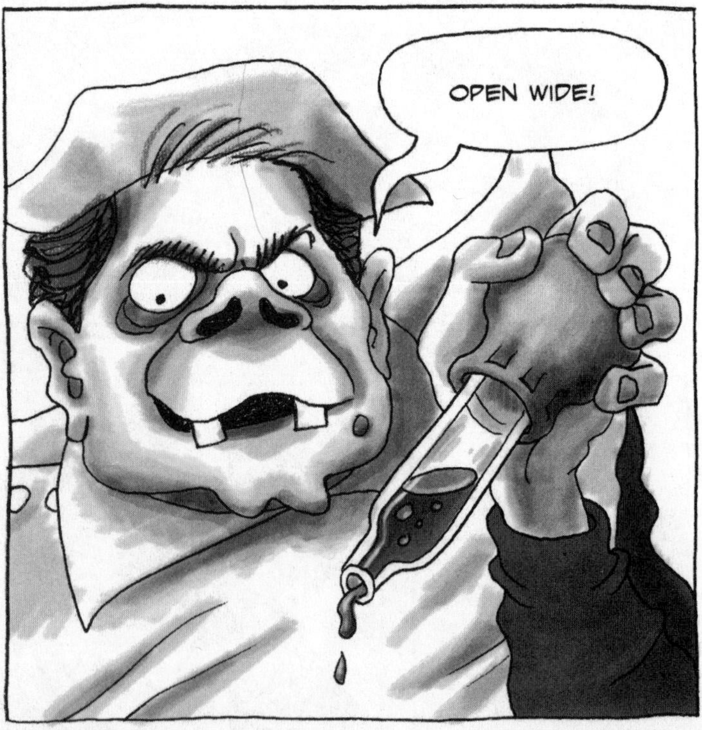
OPEN WIDE!

Nurse Bilgewater chuckled. "It's tastee-licious, and good for you, too. Guzzle it on down, there's my good little brat."

"I'm not your little brat! I . . ." *Glug.*

Nurse Bilgewater took advantage of Cody's open mouth to blast him with eight ounces of stinking slime. He spewed it out all over her dress.

"Tsk, tsk. Naughty, naughty! Cody Mack should appreciate some good wholesome fish oil. Growing up, it was like mother's milk to me."

"I'll bet," Cody said. "You let me go, you big meatball!"

"What's the trouble in here?"

It was Fronk, Howell, and Threadbare, poking their heads in the infirmary door.

"Oh, nothing," Nurse Bilgewater said. "I was just having a little fun with my patients." And before Cody could squirm away, she'd strapped a metal cuff around his ankle. The cuff was attached to a gigantic iron ball by a heavy, rusty chain. One by one, Bilgewater chained up the other boys.

Eight weeks of *this*? Would any of them

survive? And what about going to the bathroom? Never mind that. With all her crazy medical torture ideas, they'd probably all be dead long before they needed to go to the bathroom again.

And then what? She'd probably use their body parts to make new monsters! Little Frankenstein Juniors, stuck at Splurch Academy forever!

Nurse Bilgewater gestured toward the chained-up boys. "Nothing like good old-fashioned medicine. First thing the patients need," she said, "is a course of bleeding." She reached for a jar labeled LEECHES on one of her shelves.

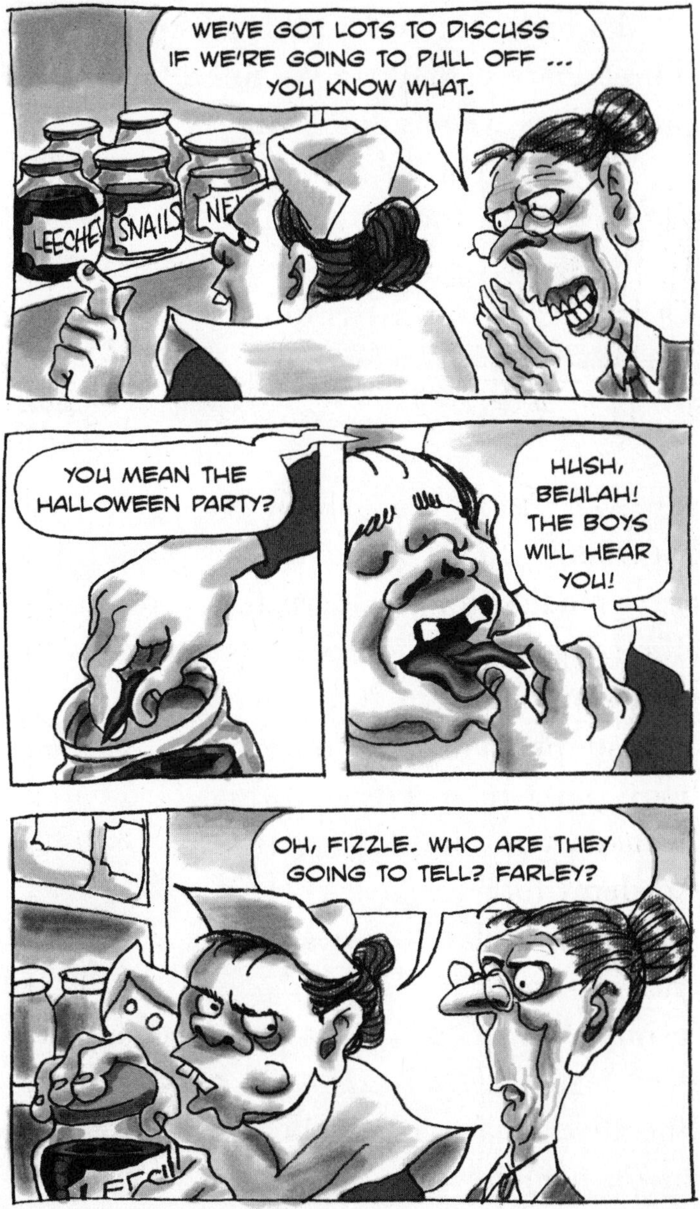
WE'VE GOT LOTS TO DISCUSS IF WE'RE GOING TO PULL OFF ... YOU KNOW WHAT.
LEECHES
SNAILS
YOU MEAN THE HALLOWEEN PARTY?
HUSH, BEULAH! THE BOYS WILL HEAR YOU!
OH, FIZZLE. WHO ARE THEY GOING TO TELL? FARLEY?

"Farley's not our problem now," Miss Threadbare said. "We've got to focus on party plans. Who's doing what?"

"I'm doing food," Bilgewater said. "Little Boy Shish Kebabs? Cream of Crud-faced Brat? No, get this. Sauteed Organs of Disruptive Students. Yum!"

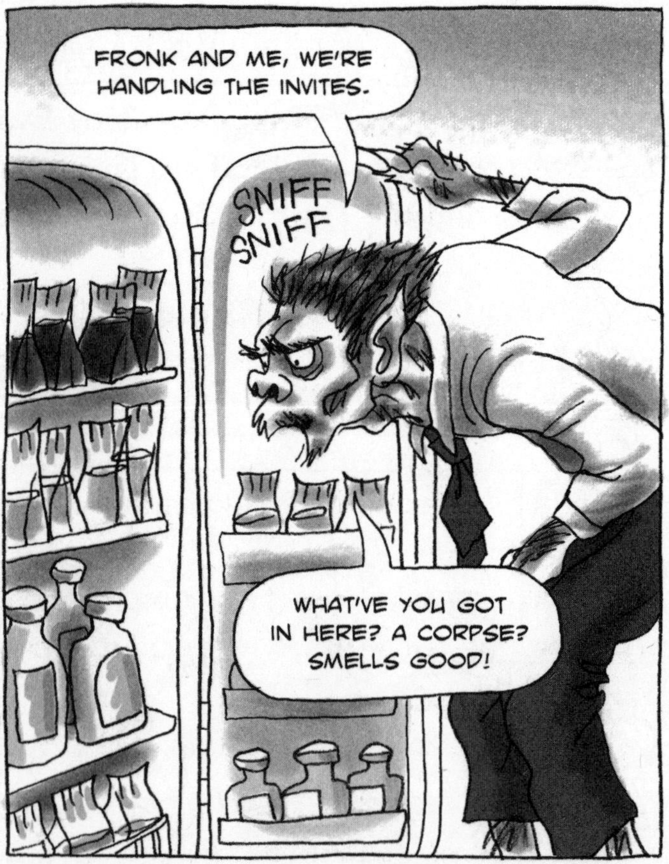
FRONK AND ME, WE'RE HANDLING THE INVITES.
SNIFF SNIFF
WHAT'VE YOU GOT IN HERE? A CORPSE? SMELLS GOOD!

"No corpses. Medical stuff. Back off," Nurse Bilgewater said.

Howell opened a jar of floating eyeballs and snagged one with his tongue. "So we got guests, and we got food," he said. "What else do we need?"

"We need plenty," Miss Threadbare said. "Decorations. Entertainment. Games."

"Simple," Howell said. "Decorate the party with little boys. Make them sing and dance to entertain us. Then, for a game, let them loose, and the first monsters to catch them get to eat them."

"I love it when their little eyeballs go *pop*," Fronk said. "That's the best part about eating a head."

Miss Threadbare giggled. "It's tempting, Prometheus," she said. "But we did promise to behave."

Mr. Fronk stretched his arms. "We're monsters," he said. "Since when do we keep promises?"

CHAPTER FOUR

THE KEY

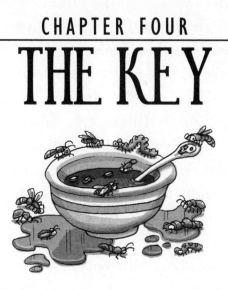

Cody was starving. The stolen snacks had worn off hours ago. He had to go to the bathroom so badly, he figured he was turning yellow.

His ankle was sore and raw from tugging at the iron cuff. And he'd thought this rotten place couldn't get any worse. He needed to bust out! If only he could mind-control a trained hawk to smash through the windows and peck out Nurse Bilgewater's eyes. Or blow up his chains with a motion-activated percussion bomb. Or teleport to another dimension.

But if he could do any of those things, he'd have ditched Splurch Academy for Disruptive Boys a *long* time before this.

The door to the infirmary opened. In came Nurse Bilgewater and Griselda. Each carried trays of foul-smelling liquid in bowls, and slabs of dry, moldy bread.

"Cabbage soup tonight," Bilgewater announced. "Everyone's special favorite. Don't anybody say I don't take good care of the patients in my infirmary! Eat up."

She passed out the soup bowls and spoons.

The soup was swimming with floating dead bug bodies. The boys were so hungry—and so used to the disgusting food served at Splurch Academy—that they almost didn't care. They dug in and ate—all but Ratface. He looked like he didn't know how to eat.

Nurse Bilgewater scowled at Ratface, tapping her toes impatiently, but he only sat there like a confused lump.

"Don't be all day about it, boy," she told Ratface. "I've got better things to do than wait for you to eat."

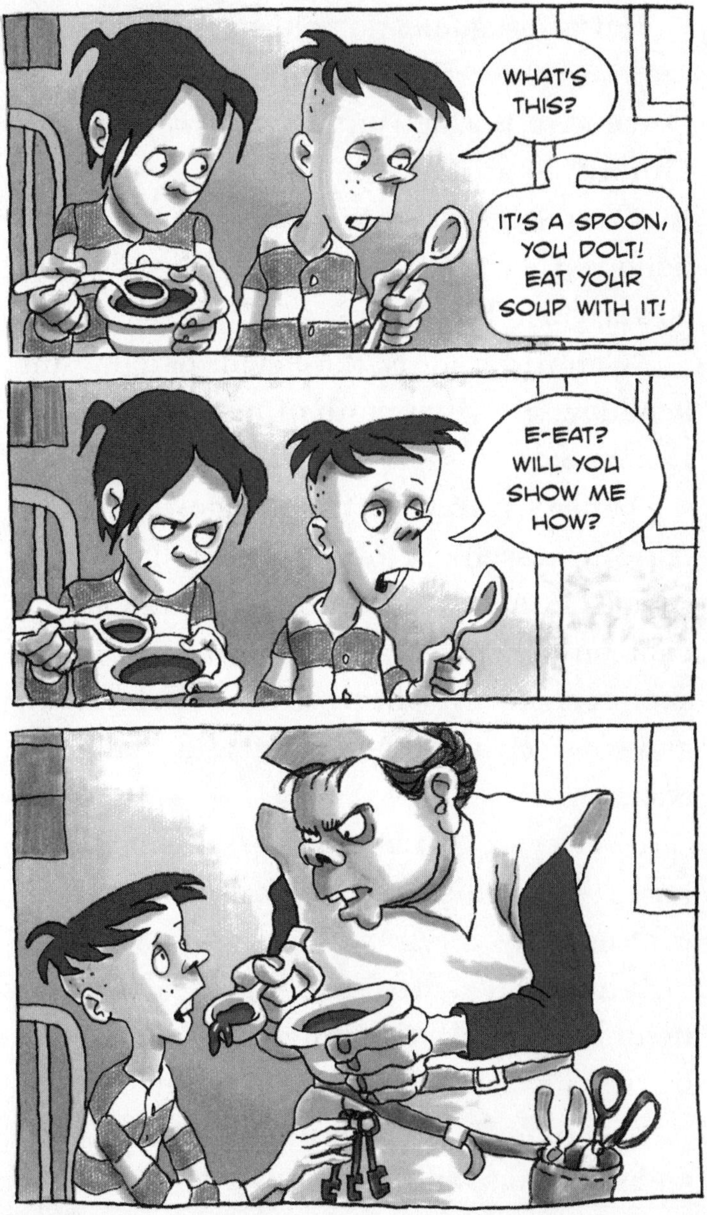
WHAT'S THIS?
IT'S A SPOON, YOU DOLT! EAT YOUR SOUP WITH IT!
E-EAT? WILL YOU SHOW ME HOW?

Ratface gagged and spluttered. The soup ran down his chin and onto his prison suit. Some of it splashed onto Nurse Bilgewater's uniform.

"You'll get no more soup tonight!" she bellowed. "Serves you right! Idiots would all starve, if I had my say."

"Yes, ma'am," Ratface said, hanging his head low. He sat on both of his hands. What was he *doing*?

"That's funny," Nurse Bilgewater said, patting herself all over. "I just had those keys. Didn't I?" She looked under the cots, on the shelves, in her armpits. Finally she stormed into her office and returned, gnawing on a candy bar and dangling another set of keys.

"Let's go, Grizzy," Nurse Bilgewater said. "These disruptive sickies can rot here till tomorrow."

They turned off the light. The door shut behind them. If the infirmary was creepy by day, it was way creepier at night.

Suddenly, Cody heard noises. Rustlings, and clinkings, and footsteps! Who was out to get them now? They were lying there helpless, like bait! Was the faculty coming back in their monster shapes to eat the kids?

Then someone whispered in his ear. "Hang on a sec, Cody, and I'll get you out of here."

The lock sprang open at his ankle. The cuff clattered to the floor.

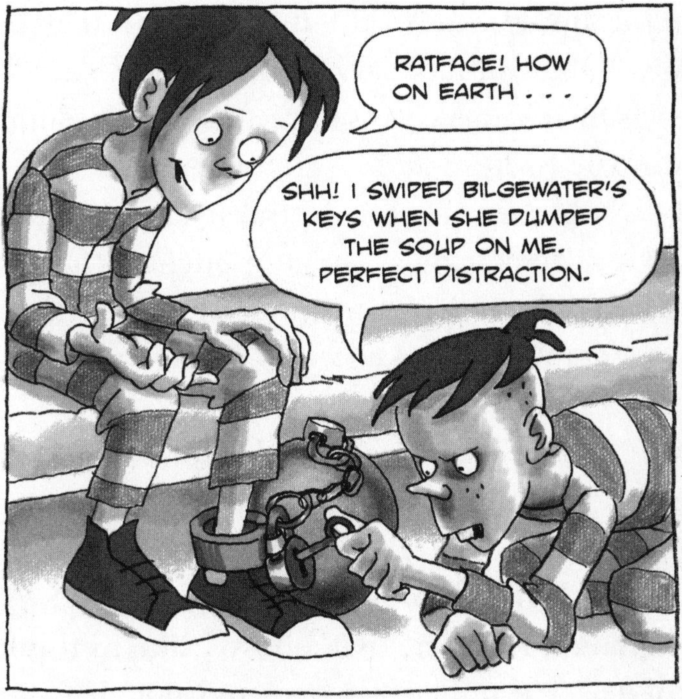
RATFACE! HOW ON EARTH . . .
SHH! I SWIPED BILGEWATER'S KEYS WHEN SHE DUMPED THE SOUP ON ME. PERFECT DISTRACTION.

Victor tumbled off his cot, moaning and rubbing his ankle. "Thanks, man."

[redacted]

Carlos was next. "Ratface, you're my hero," he said.

"A thieving genius!" Cody added.

"I'm going to call you Harry Houdini from now on," Sully said.

"Why, what did I ever do to you?" Ratface said.

"It's not an insult," Sully said. "Harry Houdini was a world famous escape artist."

"Oh," Ratface said. "In that case, sure."

Once Mugsy was set free, he went straight for the fridge.

"Oh, man, am I thirsty," he said. "Hey, look, guys. Juice pouches! Looks like apple and tomato juice. Figures those teachers would keep all the good stuff hidden for themselves."

"I hate tomato juice," Victor said. "My granddad drinks it. It's gross."

"Here then. Take apple," Mugsy said. "I don't mind tomato juice. It's like runny ketchup. At least, that's how I like to think of it." He pulled his own red pouch from the fridge. "Hmm, there's no straw. Only one way in, I guess."

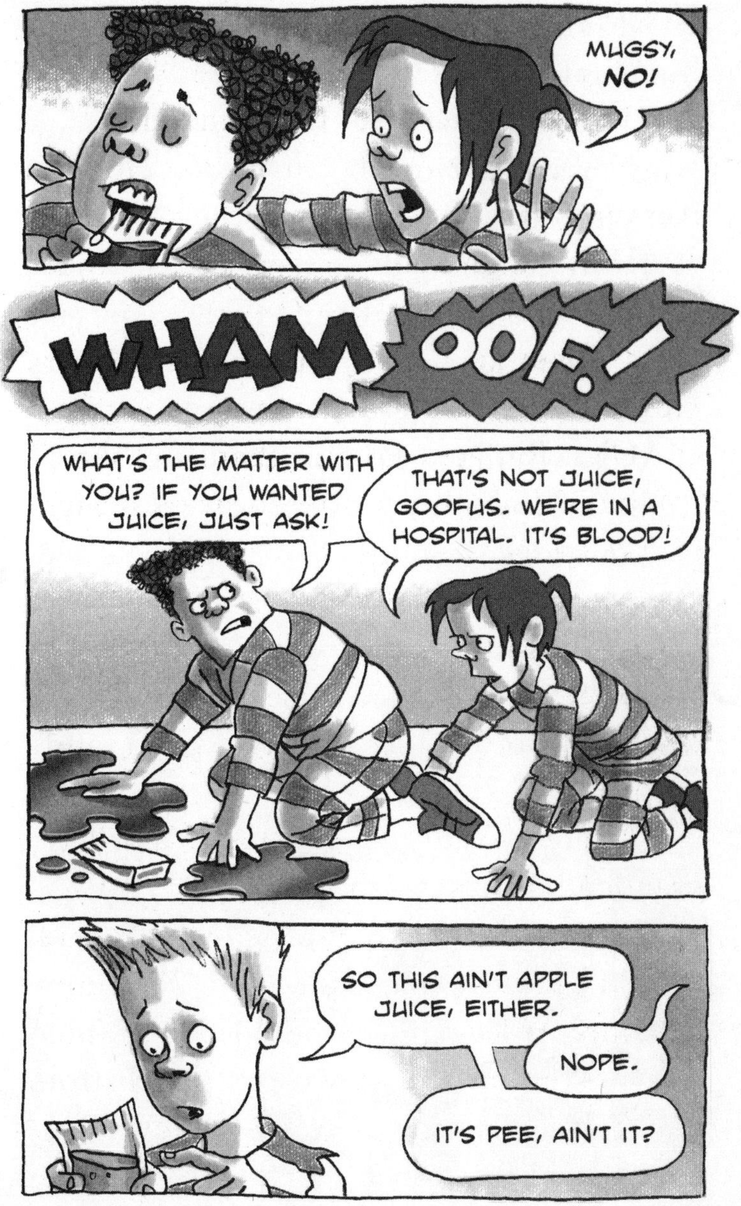
MUGSY, NO!
WHAM
OOF!
WHAT'S THE MATTER WITH YOU? IF YOU WANTED JUICE, JUST ASK!
THAT'S NOT JUICE, GOOFUS. WE'RE IN A HOSPITAL. IT'S BLOOD!
SO THIS AIN'T APPLE JUICE, EITHER.
NOPE.
IT'S PEE, AIN'T IT?

"'Fraid so," Cody said. "How much did you drink?"

Victor was shaking. "None, yet," he said. "But I was real close."

"Well, no harm done then," Ratface said. "What're we going to do now?"

"You've got a full set of keys, haven't you?" Cody asked. "Let's bust out of here for good!"

Victor pumped his fist in the air. "Yeah! Right out the front door!"

"Sayonara Splurch!" Carlos cried. "Hasta la vista!"

"I'm awesome! I'm awesome!" Ratface chanted. "I'm the hero! I'm the hero!"

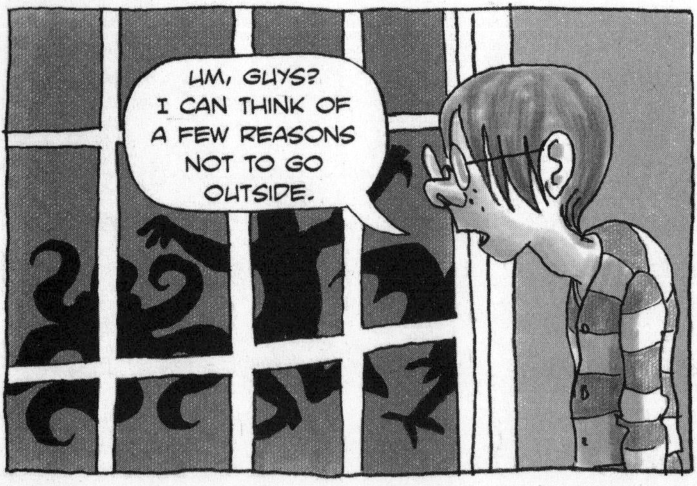
UM, GUYS? I CAN THINK OF A FEW REASONS NOT TO GO OUTSIDE.

An unearthly shriek pierced the night air. It wasn't a bird.

They gathered around the window and gazed out at the dark, shifting shadows on the grounds below.

It was their teachers, in their true shapes.

Monsters.

Werewolves. Frankensteins. Sickening mutants.

Roaming the grounds and hunting for prey. Just like every night.

"We'd never get past them," Carlos said. "Not in a million years."

Something thumped against the glass, and they all jumped.

"It's only a bat," Sully said, but that didn't stop him from shaking.

"Look at this! Look! Look!" Cody looked over to see Mugsy buried waist-deep in a cupboard in Nurse Bilgewater's office.

They pulled Mugsy out by his ankles and looked inside the cupboard. There, swarming with bugs, were dozens upon dozens of bags of Halloween candy!

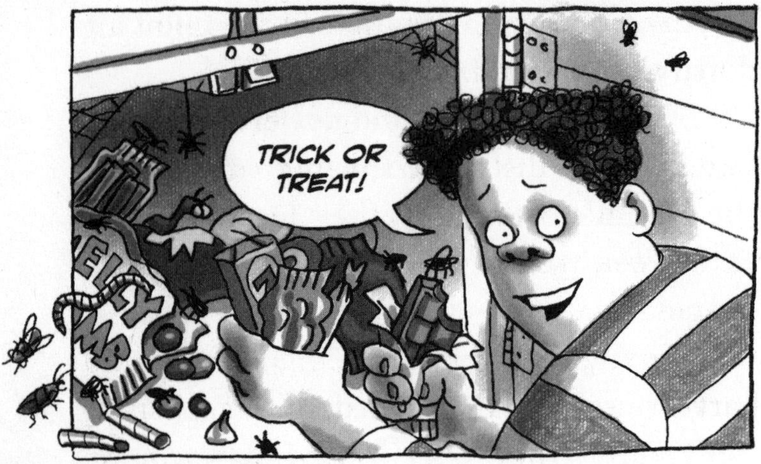
TRICK OR TREAT!

"I call the Nutty Nougat Nubs!" Carlos said as he grabbed a handful of candy.

"Gimme that Caramelly Belly Bomb," Victor said. "I saw it first!"

"Then give me the Tart & Tangy Lickety Stix," Carlos said. "You can share, but I warn you, I double dip."

"Sugar," Mugsy sighed. "Beautiful sugar . . . happy sugar . . . I died and went to sugar heaven . . ."

They sat there for hours, sorting through

the candy, picking out the bugs, chowing down till their stomachs ached.

"There's still some candy left," Ratface said. "Do we just leave it here?"

"I'll bet it's for the teacher's big Halloween party," Cody said. "Didn't they say Bilgewater was in charge of the food?"

"What's with them and their stupid old party, anyway?" Victor said.

"I think they only locked us away so we wouldn't interfere with their party," Sully said.

"Then I say we interfere," Cody said.

The boys all looked at Cody, wide-eyed.

"Are you serious?" Sully shook his head. "They'll slaughter us!"

"No, they won't," Cody said. "They're not allowed."

"Yeah!" Carlos said. "Let's do it. Let's booby-trap 'em!"

Cody picked up Nurse Bilgewater's keys and jingled them.

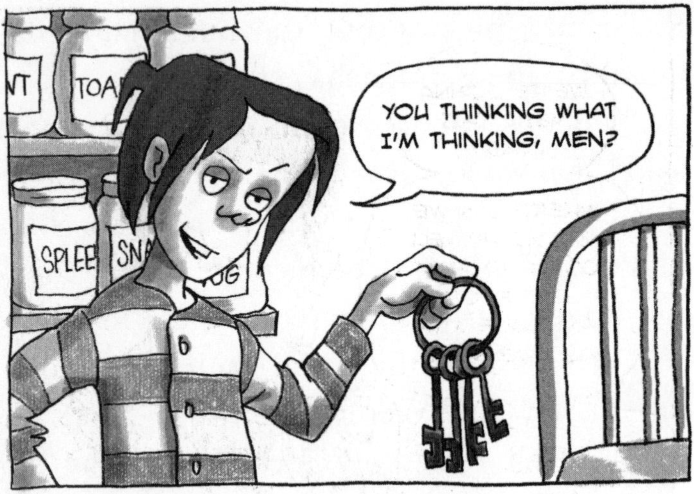
YOU THINKING WHAT I'M THINKING, MEN?

Ratface rubbed his hands together. "Time for a little exploring."

"Right." Cody looked at the clock. "I think we've got about another hour before the teachers come inside and go to bed."

"We could look for stuff to make booby traps," Carlos said. "The science rooms, the art room . . ."

"Griselda's kitchen," Mugsy added.

"Farley's lab," Ratface said.

"While we're at it, let's find stuff to make our own costumes," Carlos said. "After we sabotage their party, let's have our own."

"Yeah!"

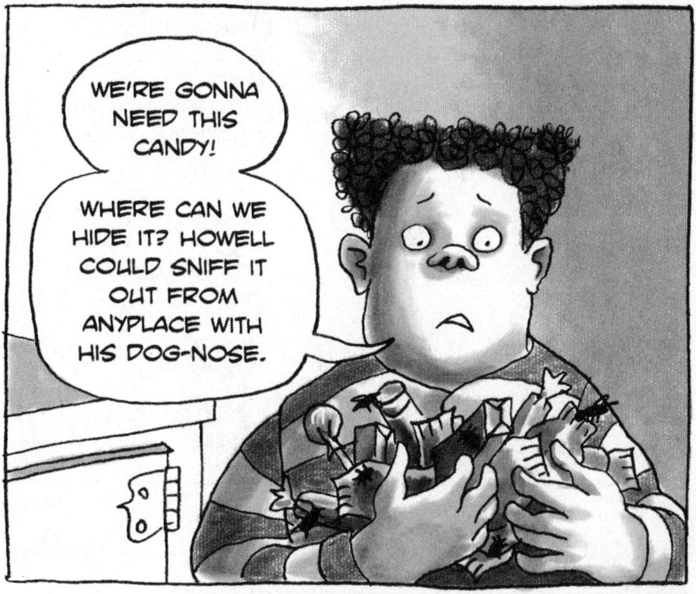
WE'RE GONNA NEED THIS CANDY!
WHERE CAN WE HIDE IT? HOWELL COULD SNIFF IT OUT FROM ANYPLACE WITH HIS DOG-NOSE.

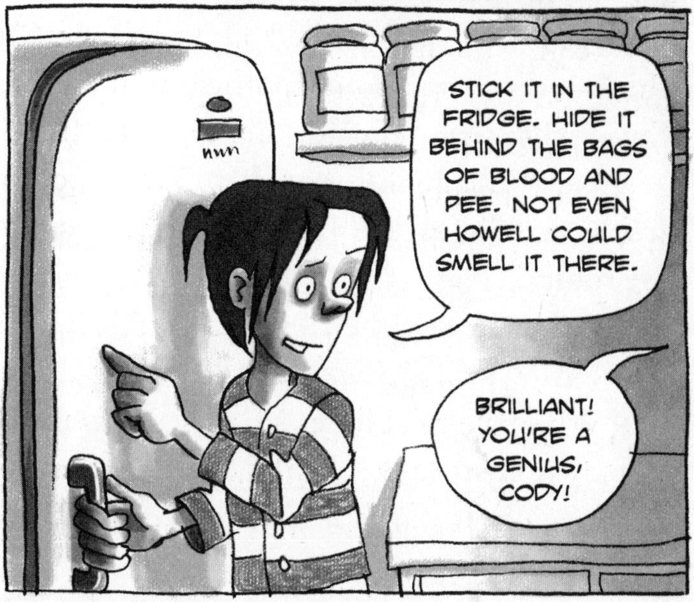
STICK IT IN THE FRIDGE. HIDE IT BEHIND THE BAGS OF BLOOD AND PEE. NOT EVEN HOWELL COULD SMELL IT THERE.
BRILLIANT! YOU'RE A GENIUS, CODY!

"Aw, it was nothing," Cody said. "I do that kind of thing all the time."

They took off down the hall, tiptoeing so Ivanov, the hunchbacked hall monitor, wouldn't hear them. They could only pray that Pavlov, the gigantic devil dog, wouldn't smell them.

"Where to now?" Victor asked.

"First stop, the library," Sully said.

"The *what*?"

"I need to go to the library," Sully said. "If we have to die of boredom sitting around here all day, at least I can read."

"Yeah, but this library doesn't have any comic books," Ratface said. "What are you going to read?"

They reached the library and slipped inside. It smelled like old, dusty paper. Sully, who spent more time here than any other boy, went right to the shelf he wanted. "I'll read the perfect Halloween book," he said, holding up a cover that looked awfully similar to the one face Cody never wanted to see again.

"I'll read *Dracula*."

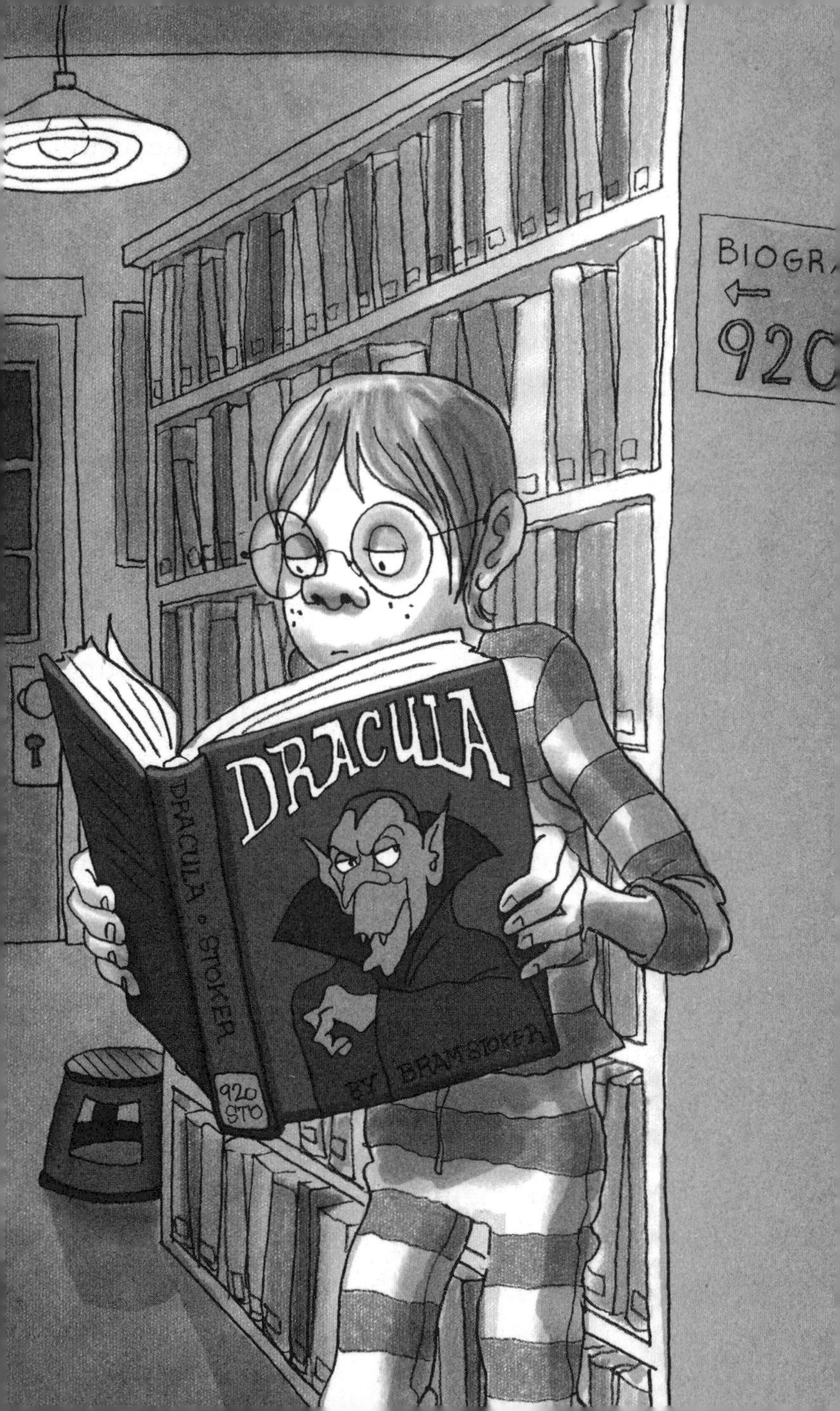
BIOGRA
920
DRACULA
DRACULA • STOKER
920 STO
BY BRAM STOKER

They dragged a protesting Sully away from the library and rampaged all over the school, looting it of anything useful they could find that might help them make costumes or booby traps.

"Don't make too much of a mess or they'll suspect us!" Sully chewed on his fingernails.

"Are you kidding?" Ratface was busy gnawing on a stolen doughnut from Griselda's kitchen. "We're locked up in the infirmary! We've got the perfect alibi. If anything, they'll blame kids from the other grades."

"Get a bunch of eggs," Carlos instructed. "In a few days they'll be the best stink bombs *ever*."

"Guys," Sully pleaded. "Seriously. We're really pushing our luck. Let's get back to the infirmary. They're gonna come back inside any minute. If we're not in bed . . ." He drew a finger across his throat.

"Aw, quit being such a worrywart," Victor said. "We're starving. I'm not leaving until I eat."

Then they all froze. They heard a sound. A low, menacing growl, and a hobbling tread.

"I hear 'em, boy." It was Ivanov, the hall monitor, addressing Pavlov, the Hound of Death. "Students out of bed at night. Let's get to the dormitories and give 'em a taste of your medicine."

Cody beckoned to the other boys. "Grab your stuff and let's go," he whispered, barely louder than the sound of breathing. "They're going to the dorms first. It's our only chance." And, taking a different hallway, they scurried back to the infirmary, hid their loot, locked up their ankles once more, and threw themselves down onto their bunks and, soon, into an uneasy sleep.

CHAPTER FIVE
THE BUG

Cody's eyes flew open.

He was in the dungeon, slumped on the dirty floor!

Did he sleepwalk here? He *had* been asleep. He was sure of it. He remembered settling down to sleep on his cot in the infirmary, after the boys finished their raid of the Academy. Ratface had locked them back into their chains, and hid the keys in his underpants. Rasputin had snuggled down with him like always.

So what was Cody doing here?

And how did he get out of his chains?

Cody had been here before. There was the ancient furnace, wheezing in the corner, with pipes and vents coming out in every direction. It looked like a giant steel amoeba. Rats scuttled along the floor, and bugs! Bugs were everywhere, swarming all over his skin. *Ugh!* Long bugs, short bugs, bugs with six legs, and bugs with a million. Good thing Cody wasn't squeamish or he'd be freaking right out of his skin.

Something scuttled in the darkness at his feet. A rat. Rasputin. Cody could tell. He was nosing around in a dark corner, sniffing. Suddenly he hissed and squeaked.

Bzzzrrrrzzz. Bzzzrrrrzzz.

Cody knelt for a closer look. Something was in that corner, making a rattling noise, and whatever it was, Rasputin looked ready to attack it.

It wasn't another rat. He hoped it wasn't a rattlesnake.

Rasputin snapped at the thing, and a long, shiny something lashed back. Rasputin backed away, squeaking. The thing waddled after him.

Bzzzrrrzzz.

Cody's jaw fell open. The buzzing, rattling thing was a *beetle*! The hugest bug Cody had ever seen, even bigger than the rat! Dripping with slime, it had thin wings streaked with veins poking out from under its thick black shell of a body. And scaly, menacing pincers stuck out of its head and snapped at Rasputin!

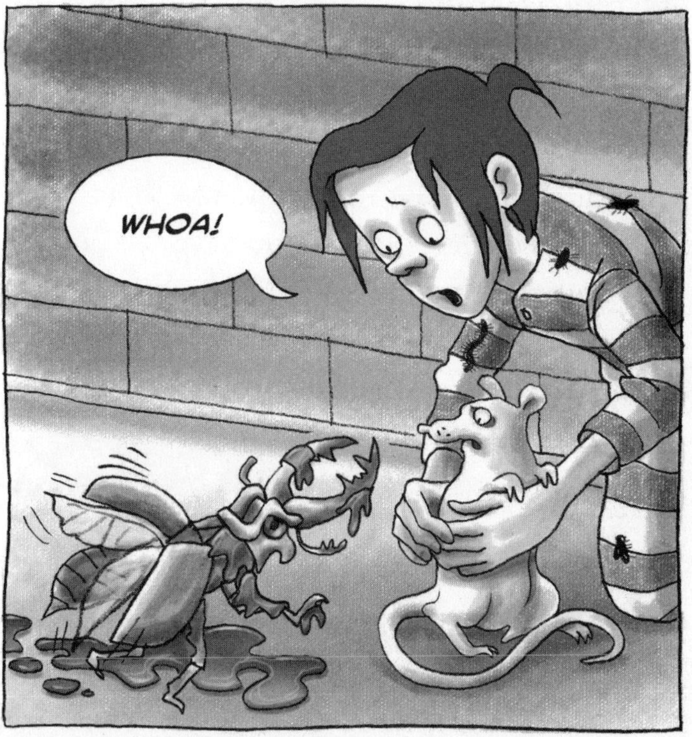
WHOA!

Cody scooped up his adopted pet. "Hey!" he yelled. "Leave my rat alone!"

He raised a foot to stomp on the bug, and wondered if he'd even be able to put a dent in it, much less squoosh it. But before he could slam his foot down, Rasputin nipped Cody's ear.

"Ow!"

Cody's yell echoed through the dungeon. Rasputin clambered off Cody and onto the floor, where he watched the beetle from a cautious distance.

Cody bent down for a closer look. Carefully, he took hold of the beetle. It turned its antlered head and glared at him.

"You oughtta be on TV," he said. "You look a million years old."

The beetle released a jet of stink.

BLECH! YOU'RE A STINK BEETLE!

Suddenly, at the top of the stairs, a door opened. The beam of a flashlight moved around the dungeon.

"Who goes there?" the crackly voice of Ivanov, the hall monitor, said. Pavlov growled a murderous warning.

Cody set down the bug, slunk back into the shadows, and held his breath. Bugs crawled across his feet and up his pant legs. They climbed over his ears and down into the soft tickly neck parts below his collar. He shuddered. He twitched. He caught the scream in his throat before it escaped and betrayed his position to the hall monitor and the Hound of Death, while the flashlight probed the dark corners for dungeon intruders.

The light clicked off.

"C'mon, Poochie," Ivanov said. "Must have been a rat. Let's go back to bed."

The door shut. Cody waited a few seconds longer to be sure it wasn't a trick. Then he slapped himself all over and shook bugs out of his clothes. Some bugs went crunch against his skin. *Blech!*

He followed his nose and found the bug jabbing its pincers once more at Rasputin. It still appeared to be surrounded by stinky fumes. The buzzing seemed to come from the beetle pumping its wings. There was no way those flimsy wings could get that beetle off the ground.

Oddly enough, Rasputin seemed to want to make friends with the beetle.

"You're one strange rat," Cody said, nudging Rasputin aside. He picked up the big bug once more.

"I'm keeping you," Cody said. "I found you, so I get to name you. You'll be . . . The Codius Mackittus Splurchius Beetleus."

The bug flailed its long scraggly legs. They felt so creepy on Cody's skin, he nearly dropped his prize.

"I want a better look at you," Cody said. "Let's find some more light." He moved to a patch where the pale light from the outdoors was a bit brighter, and held the beetle closer to his face. A cellar window acted like a mirror, letting Cody see his reflection.

Suddenly, the beetle's long, snapping pincers grew longer and longer, stretching out like salad tongs to grab Cody's neck.

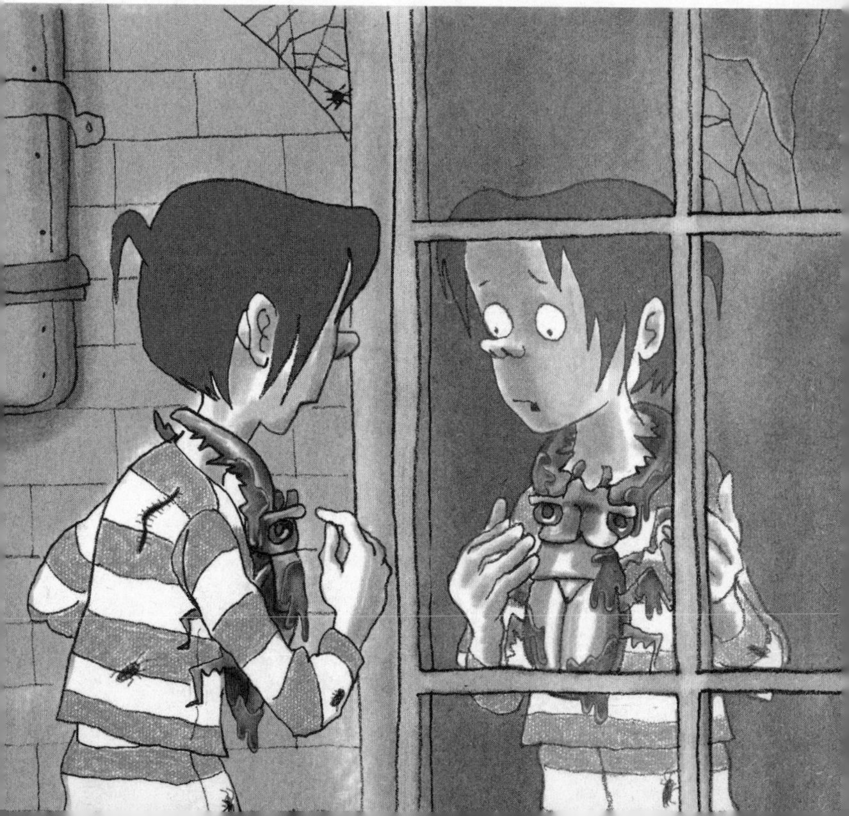

"Yee-aagh!" Cody yelped, and tried to drop the bug, but he couldn't. Maybe the slime made it stick. Its pincers clamped themselves all the way around Cody's neck and fastened together in the back, until the beetle hung around his neck like a giant, heavy necklace. And the beetle! The beetle itself got heavier and heavier, yet it got smaller and smaller. Its body now glowed with a dull shine. Cody cautiously tapped a fingernail against it. It was hard, and cold.

"Gold," Cody whispered. "You turned into *gold*!"

Rasputin leaped onto Cody's shoulder and leaned down around his neck, sniffing at the golden beetle.

"What do you make of that, Rasputin?" Cody said. "He doesn't stink anymore, does he? But he weighs a ton."

Outside the window, the sky began to turn lavender. Morning was here.

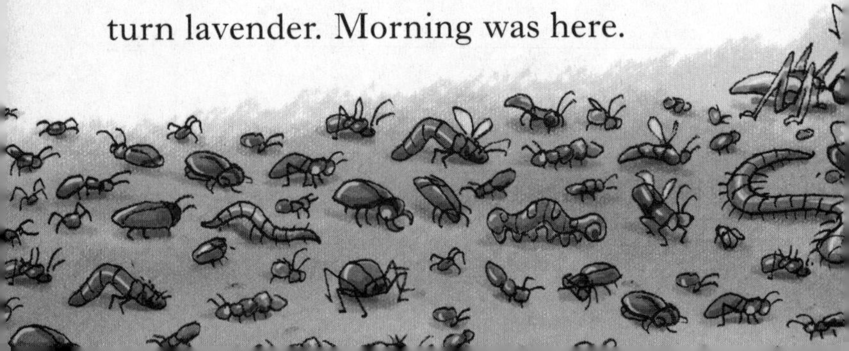

"We'd better scoot back to the infirmary before Nurse Bilgewater comes searching for me," Cody told Rasputin. "I still don't know how I got out of my ball and chain, but if she finds me missing, we're toast."

And, still clutching the beetle, he crept up the stairs and through the corridors back to the infirmary.

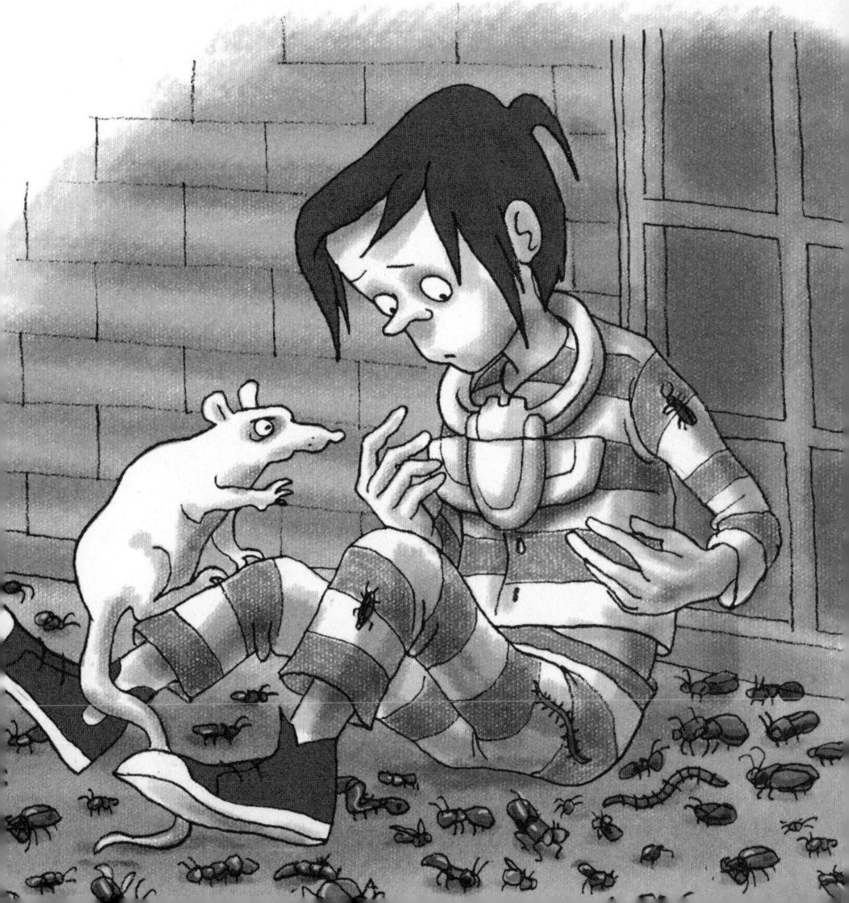

CHAPTER SIX
THE LEMONADE

"Anybody got any cheese?"

The boys all turned to look at Cody like he had a hand growing out of his head. It was midmorning, and sunlight streamed through the windows, but Cody was still lying in his bed. He'd just woken up.

"Sure, Cody," Ratface said sarcastically. "I've got a pocketful of cheese. What's the matter with you?"

"Then give me some," Cody said, holding out his hand. "I want cheese!"

Carlos snapped his fingers. "Wake up, Cody," he said. "Snap out of it."

Cody shook himself. He felt suddenly confused.

"Why are you all staring at me?"

Carlos answered first. "You were fast asleep, then you woke up begging for cheese." He shrugged. "Weird."

Cody's mouth felt dry and sticky. "Cheese?" he said. "You're joking. I don't want cheese. I want a big glass of cherry Kool-Aid."

"The blue kind's better," Ratface said.

"Nah, poison green's the best," Mugsy said. "Lime flavor, I think. Maybe pickle."

The door from the office opened, and Nurse Bilgewater filled the doorway like a monument of The Wrath of God.

"Where," she hissed, *"have you hidden my Halloween candy?"*

The boys looked at one another. Mugsy's curly hair quivered. Sully stared at the floor.

Nurse Bilgewater charged through the room, tossing the boys aside like bowling pins. She upended each cot, searching for the missing candy underneath.

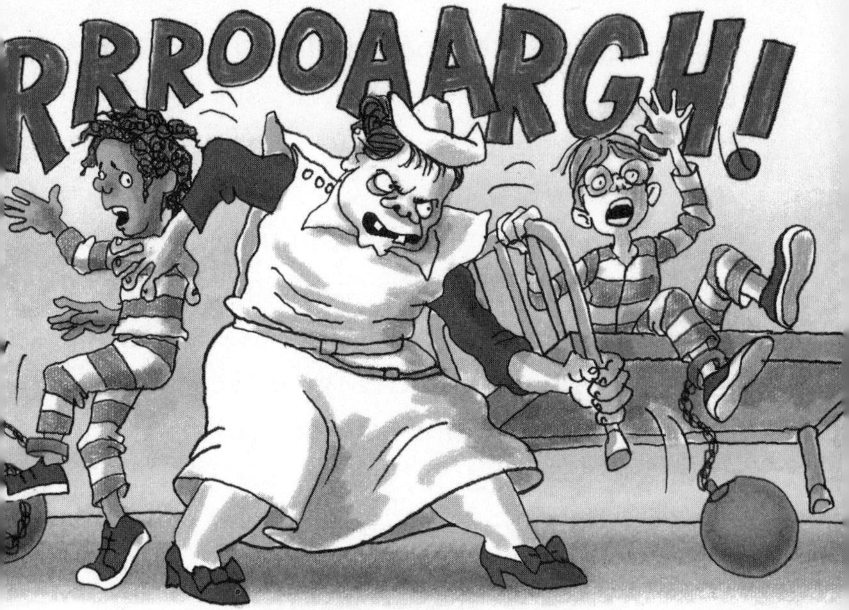
RRROOAARGH!

Windows rattled in their frames.

"Where is my CANDY?" Nurse Bilgewater bellowed.

"But . . . b-but m-ma'am," Mugsy stammered, "we were chained up all n-night. How would w-we know?"

"Don't you dare try to flimflam me, you marshmallow of a boy," Nurse Bilgewater said. "I know guilt when I smell it. And you're guilty. You're all guilty!" She jabbed a thick finger at Cody. "And you're the ringleader of the whole guilty bunch!"

She turned abruptly and returned to her office. When she reappeared, she had on a hat, coat, and gloves, and carried a purse over one arm.

"Nobody move," she said in a low voice. "I'll be back. I'd better find you all here in the exact spots where I left you, or I'll chop and boil you up into candy. See if I don't."

She shut the door behind her.

Cody lay back down on his bunk. His neck itched, and when he reached up to scratch it, there was the golden beetle. He'd forgotten about it! It had seemed like a dream. But there it was, big and heavy and strange.

"Guys, look at this," he said. The others gathered around. He told them about sleepwalking to the dungeon and finding it there, buzzing and stinking, and about how it turned to gold when he held it up to his neck.

"But . . . if you sleepwalked to the dungeon," Ratface said. "Then you must have sleep-unlocked yourself, too. That's weird."

"I know," Cody said. "I don't know how I could have gotten the key and let myself out. All I know is, I woke up in the dungeon, with Rasputin with me. He was really the one who found the beetle. It's so dark in the dungeon, and there are so many bugs, I wouldn't have seen it if Rasputin hadn't sniffed it out."

"I can't believe that thing was really alive," Sully said. "It looks like an ancient artifact. A valuable one, too."

Cody tugged at the beetle. The pincers relaxed and the gold ornament turned back into a living, squirming bug.

"Yee-ikes!" Ratface squealed. The other boys scrambled backward.

"I can't believe it's real!" Carlos said. "It's like something from a weird science show on TV."

Sully poked its armored shell. "I wonder what species it is," he said. "Could be something extinct!" He poked it once more, and the beetle released a jet of stinky spray. "Uggh!"

"Pee-yew!" Victor said.

"Geez, Mugsy," Carlos said, stifling a laugh.

Mugsy flicked Carlos's arm with his finger. "That wasn't me, and you know it, 'Los."

Cody put the bug back around his neck, and gradually the stink faded. The day went back to being Boredom City. Nothing to do but stare at the paint on the walls.

"Those rotten teachers," Cody muttered. "We've got to get back at them for locking us in here and ruining our lives just so they can plan their dumb party."

"But how?" Mugsy said. "If we let ourselves out, they'll see us and take away our key."

Cody ground his teeth. "There must be something we could do."

"Hey, guys," Victor said, peeking out the infirmary door's window. "What's Griselda doing, across the hall?"

They crowded around the window for a better look.

Across the hall was a room with a fireplace and a fancy table. Through the doorway they could see Griselda setting a table.

"That used to be Farley's private study,"
Ratface said. "Now the teachers use it as
their luxury dining room."

"I'll bet Farley wouldn't be too happy to
know they're using it," Carlos said.

"His bedroom is right next door,"
Ratface said. "I know every room in this
entire place."

"Quit bragging," Victor said. "I don't
want to know any rooms in this stupid
place."

"Farley's room, eh?" Cody said. "Now there's a room I'd like to explore. Who knows what kind of weird junk he keeps in his dresser drawers, huh?"

"Maybe a secret map showing all the escape routes out of this place," Carlos said.

"Maybe the keys to the hidden treasure chests," Ratface said. "I'll bet there's gold!"

"Maybe the codes for the bombs that could blow this place sky-high," Victor grumbled. "You guys are nuts."

"I'm thirsty," Mugsy said. "And starving. When are they ever going to feed us?"

"Griselda's back," Sully whispered. "Shh."

They looked out the window again. She'd placed a tray containing covered plates and tall drinks on a table in the hallway.

"Lemonade!" Mugsy cried. "I haven't had lemonade since before I came to Splurch!"

"Tough luck," Victor said.

"Gimme that key," Mugsy said. "I'm going to get me some lemonade."

"And get us all caught?" Ratface said. "No way."

"C'mon, Ratface," Cody said, "where's your sense of adventure? I've got an idea." He opened the refrigerator. "We're all going to have a drink of lemonade. And we're going to leave a little present for our *beloved* teachers."

He loaded up his pockets with pouches. Griselda took the tray into the private dining room and set the glasses around the table.

Then, muttering to herself, she hobbled back down the hall with her tray toward the kitchens.

As soon as she was out of sight, Cody unlocked the door.

"Ssssh!" He put a finger over his mouth to signal to the others. Then slowly, carefully, they tiptoed across the hall.

"Drink up, men," he said, grabbing for the first glass. "Just leave an inch in the bottom of the glass."

"Huh?" Ratface said.

"Trust me."

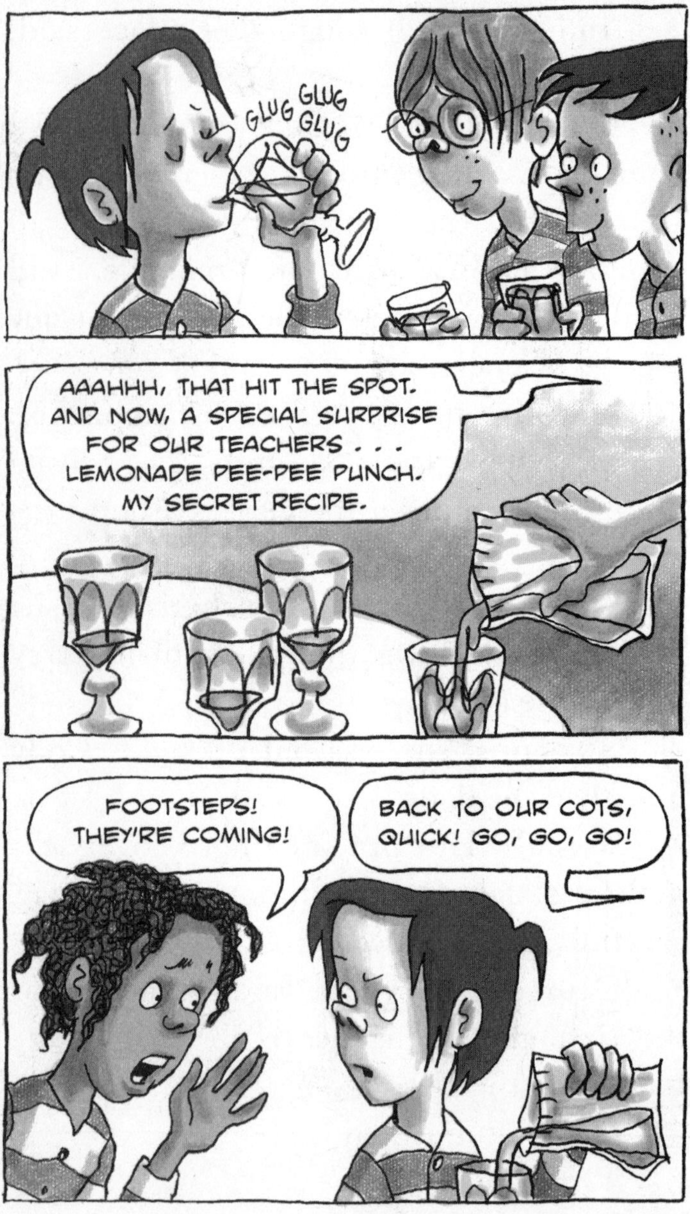
GLUG GLUG
GLUG
AAAHHH, THAT HIT THE SPOT. AND NOW, A SPECIAL SURPRISE FOR OUR TEACHERS . . . LEMONADE PEE-PEE PUNCH. MY SECRET RECIPE.
FOOTSTEPS! THEY'RE COMING!
BACK TO OUR COTS, QUICK! GO, GO, GO!

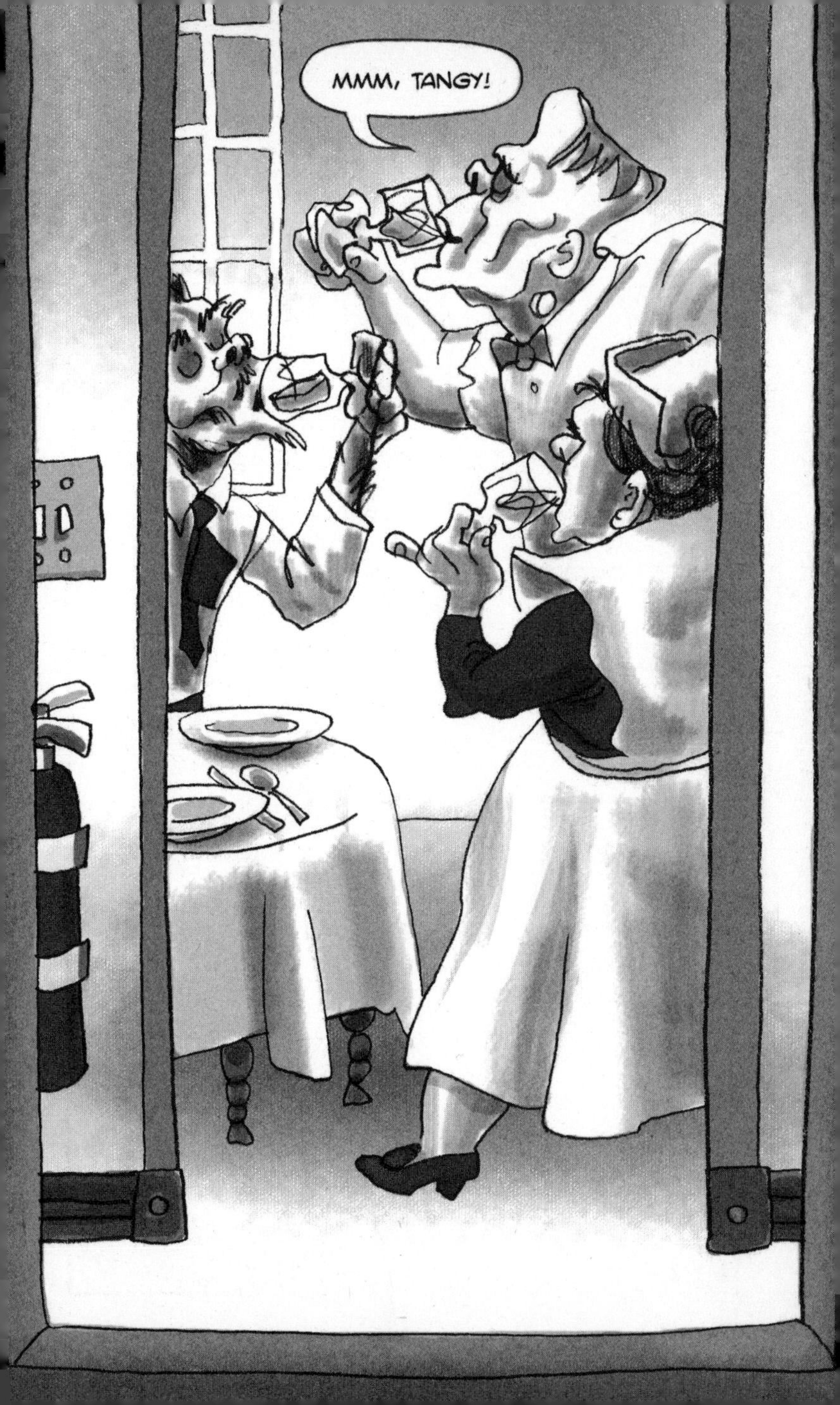
MMM, TANGY!

CHAPTER SEVEN

THE TIME CAPSULE

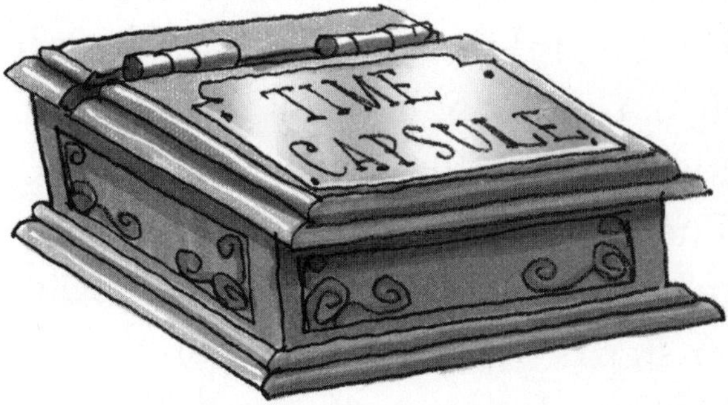
TIME
CAPSULE

That night, after they were sure the teachers had gone out for their moonlight romp on the grounds of the Academy, Cody and the boys helped themselves to sacks of candy from Nurse Bilgewater's hidden stash (she kept on buying more), then let themselves out of the infirmary and tiptoed to Headmaster Farley's bedroom. They had decided that was where they would plan their party and make their costumes. After all, no one would disturb them there.

The room smelled like mothballs and bad breath, but looked pretty much like a normal bedroom—Splurch style, that is. All the furniture had carvings of gargoyles.

"Ugh, did Farley ever actually sleep here?" Carlos said. "Gross!"

"No, stupid," Sully said, waving his copy of *Dracula* in his face. "Vampires sleep in coffins. You know he went out every night hunting for . . . whatever he hunts for."

They searched through his drawers, but all they found were old black socks and boxer shorts with pink hearts on them.

"Ew," Ratface pinched his nose. "Farley's undies? Too much information."

Carlos dumped out the bag of art supply junk they'd collected the night before. "Time to plan our own Halloween," he said. "Let's make costumes."

"We've got more to do than just costumes," Victor said. "We've gotta make booby traps and get back at those rotten teachers for locking us up so they can have their crummy party."

"I saved a bag of dead bugs," Mugsy said. "From when we were eating the candy before. They'll make a great booby trap."

"Good thinking," Ratface said. "Our eggs should be getting good and rotten by now. We'll drop 'em from the upstairs windows."

"And I'll dump the bugs into the punch," Mugsy said.

"No, wait," Carlos said. "I'll make a spring-loaded booby trap launcher. Then we can shoot the bugs and eggs and stuff out onto the party."

"Speaking of bugs," Sully said, as he poked at Cody's neck. "You've got a rash or something on your neck that looks pretty bad."

The boys all crowded around to see.

"Looks like some kinda bite," Mugsy said. "Like when I get bug bites at summer camp—when I *used to* go to summer camp—they'd swell up and get gross."

"Bug bites," Cody repeated. He tapped his golden beetle thoughtfully. "Suppose this beetle thing is biting me?"

"Do necklaces bite?" Carlos asked.

"It's not always a necklace," Cody said.

"I wouldn't wear it if I were you," Sully said. "Some huge hocus-pocus like that's gotta be bad news."

Cody shrugged. "Who knows? Maybe it's a disease called Splurchivitis."

"*Any*way," Carlos said, peeling open a candy bar, "what are we going to be for Halloween?"

"Simple," Cody said. "We need to dress up as monsters. It might turn out to be a useful disguise if we're going to booby-trap their party." He fingered the rashy spot on his neck. "I'll be Farley. I'll bet he's got a spare cloak in his closet I can borrow."

Cody turned the knob and pulled open the door to Farley's closet.

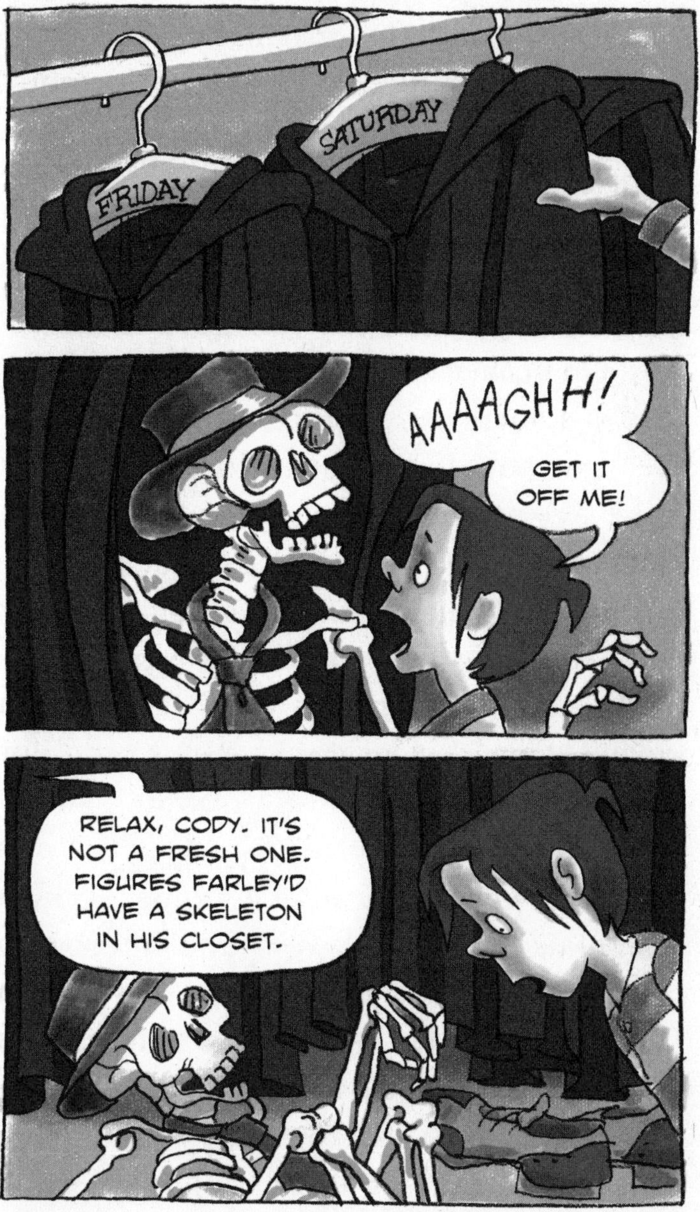
FRIDAY
SATURDAY
AAAAGHH!
GET IT OFF ME!
RELAX, CODY. IT'S NOT A FRESH ONE. FIGURES FARLEY'D HAVE A SKELETON IN HIS CLOSET.

"Yeah, but this one has a hat and tie-thingy," Cody said. "Makes it more creepy somehow."

"I call the skeleton," Victor said. "I can use it for my costume." He grabbed an arm and began moving the skeleton like a puppet, using the bony fingers to mess up Mugsy's hair. "What a nice little boy . . ." he said in a Farley-style voice.

"Knock it off," Mugsy said, swatting the hand away. "Cody, what's the matter?"

Cody was down on his hands and knees, crawling over mothballs in the dark closet. "There's something else in here," he said. "A box. It says TIME CAPSULE."

"Cool," Ratface said. "Is that like something you swallow so you'll have more time?"

Sully rolled his eyes. "Nope. It's a container you put things in. The idea is, it'll be found by future generations and they'll learn about what your life was like. Didn't you ever make one in school?"

Carlos peered over Cody's shoulder. "This is Farley's time capsule? Bust it open!"

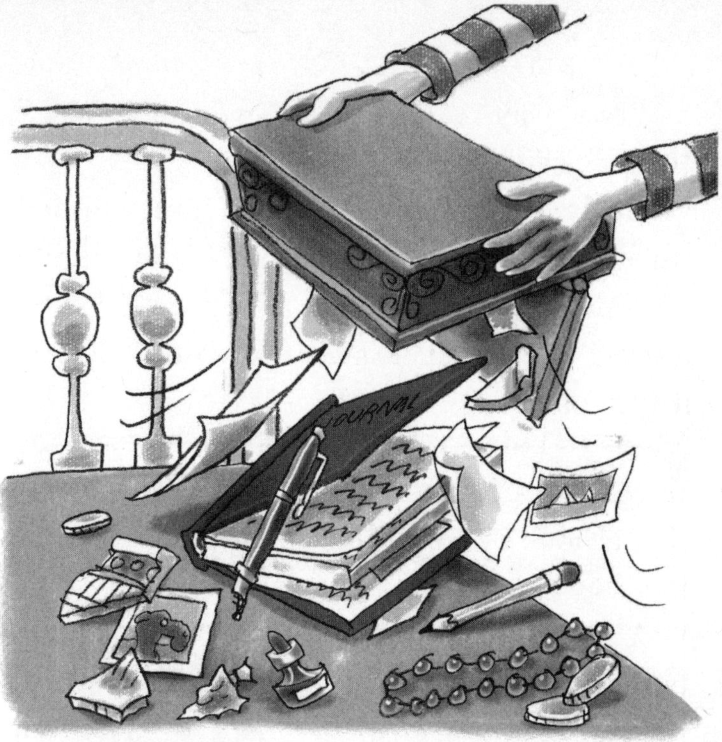
JOURNAL

They dumped the box onto the bed. At first it didn't seem like much. There were old black-and-white photographs, a book, faded bits of pottery, and some beads.

"What was he, a caveman?" Victor said, turning things over. "This looks like it's from an ancient civilization."

"Look," Sully said. "There's a photo of Farley visiting the pyramids. The back says 'Family vacation, age eleven.'" Sully looked at the other boys. "Our age."

"No way was Farley ever our age," Ratface said. "Impossible."

Sully picked up the book and flipped through the pages. "This is his journal," he said. "Hey, no way. They called him Archie back then. Listen up." Sully cleared his throat.

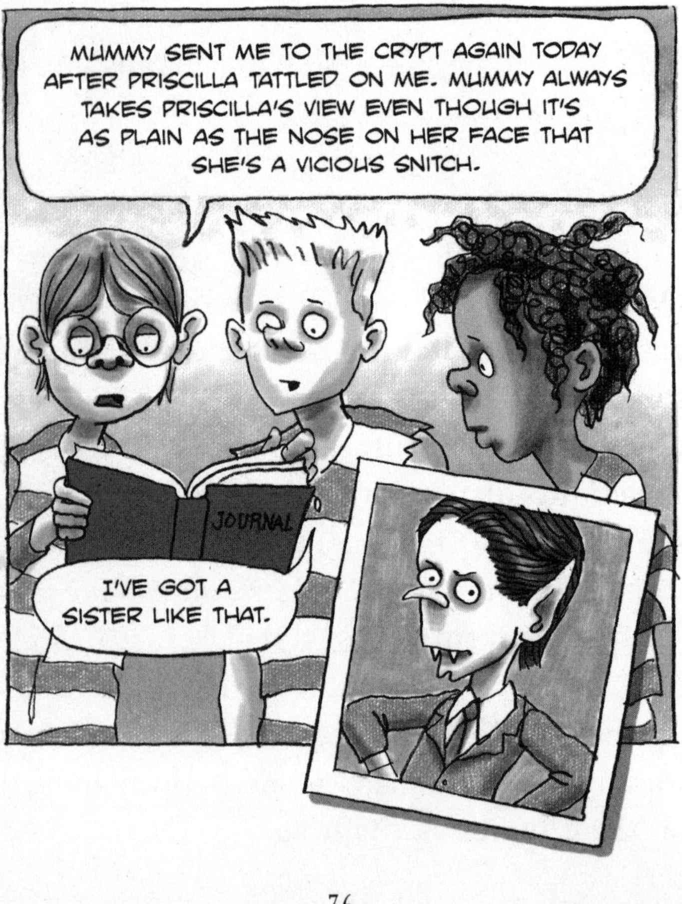
MUMMY SENT ME TO THE CRYPT AGAIN TODAY AFTER PRISCILLA TATTLED ON ME. MUMMY ALWAYS TAKES PRISCILLA'S VIEW EVEN THOUGH IT'S AS PLAIN AS THE NOSE ON HER FACE THAT SHE'S A VICIOUS SNITCH.
JOURNAL
I'VE GOT A SISTER LIKE THAT.

"'Uncle Rastus stared at me the whole time I was down there,'" Sully said, still reading from the diary. "'Priscilla said that's silly. Uncle Rastus has been dead for a long time. But something inside his eye sockets was watching me.'"

Victor suddenly stopped playing with the skeleton's arm. "Guys," he said, "I've got a feeling I've been shaking hands with Uncle Rastus."

"Get to the part about Egypt already," Cody said.

"All right, all right," Sully said. "Ahem. 'Mummy said if she had to send me to the crypt any more this week, she was going to sell my sarcophagus to a stolen antiquities dealer. Then Priscilla told Mummy I'd been sneaking out of the crypt using the back stairs, the ones leading to the cemetery.'"

"Sarcopha-what?" Carlos asked.

"Sarcophagus," Sully said. "It's a kind of coffin."

"So . . . little Archibald Farley's hobby was collecting *coffins*?" Cody said.

"Pretty much," Sully said.

Cody dusted off Uncle Rastus's hat and put it on. "And nobody thought to lock him away back then? What kind of kid collects *coffins*?"

He got up and strolled over to the window and looked down at the shadowy grounds below. A few tilting white gravestones poked up from out of the lawn like crooked teeth.

Gravestones.

Gravestones?

"Sully," Cody said, "read me that last sentence again."

"Why?"

"Just read it, okay?"

"'Priscilla told Mummy I'd been sneaking out of the crypt using the back stairs, the ones leading to the cemetery.'"

"I thought so!" Cody said. "Look. See those gravestones down there? That's the cemetery. And see that little building thingy, with the pillars and the doorway? That must be the entrance to the crypt. That's where Farley is right now, down there, underground!"

Sully didn't answer. He just looked at Cody in a funny way, then back at the book, and then at Cody once more.

"What's the matter, Sully?"

Sully put away the journal. "Oh, nothing," he said.

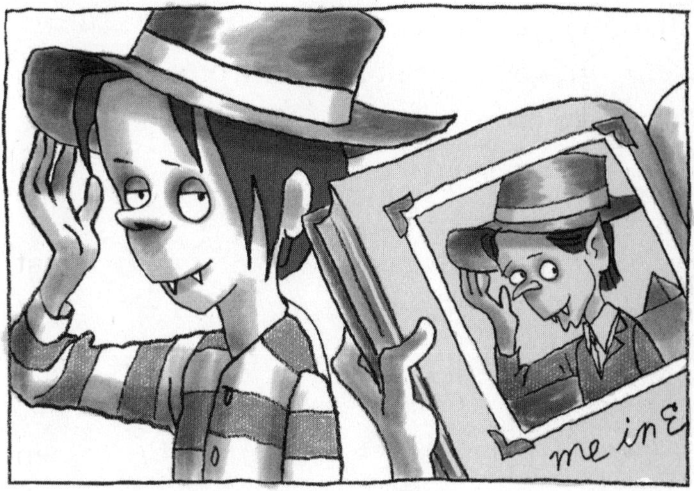
me in E

CHAPTER EIGHT
THE VAMPIRE

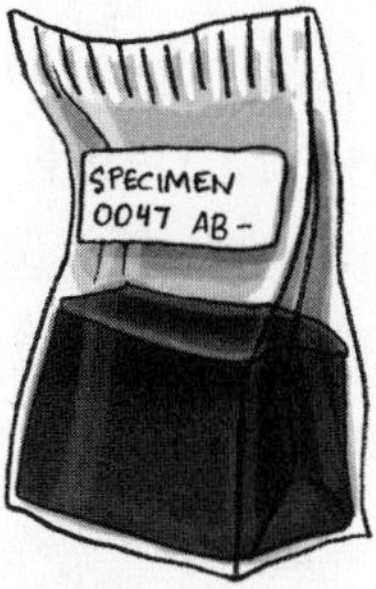
SPECIMEN
0047 AB-

Cody dreamed that night about a monster.

Not one of the monsters at the school. Those monsters seemed wimpy compared to this one. Chomping teeth, deadly eyes, and a huge, powerful body. It was quick, it was deadly, and it wore the golden beetle around its neck.

It carried a magical staff, and it whacked Cody on the head with it. It hurt, but then when it was over, Splurch Academy collapsed, and Cody's mom and dad showed up in their car to take Cody home.

"There's no place like home," Cody told his parents as they led him, skipping through a field of poppies, to their car. "There's no place like home!"

"Okay, Dorothy," a loud voice said. Something plucked him up and out of his happy dream. He blinked and opened his eyes. It was a big pair of glasses talking to him, and behind the glasses, Sully.

DUDE, WAKE UP! YOU WERE DREAMING.

He was still in the infirmary. Cody rubbed his eyes. He was thirsty. *Soooo* thirsty.

"What's the matter?" Sully asked.

"Just a weird dream." Cody replied as he slid off his cot and wandered to the sink. Water? Nah. He wanted something that would really quench his thirst.

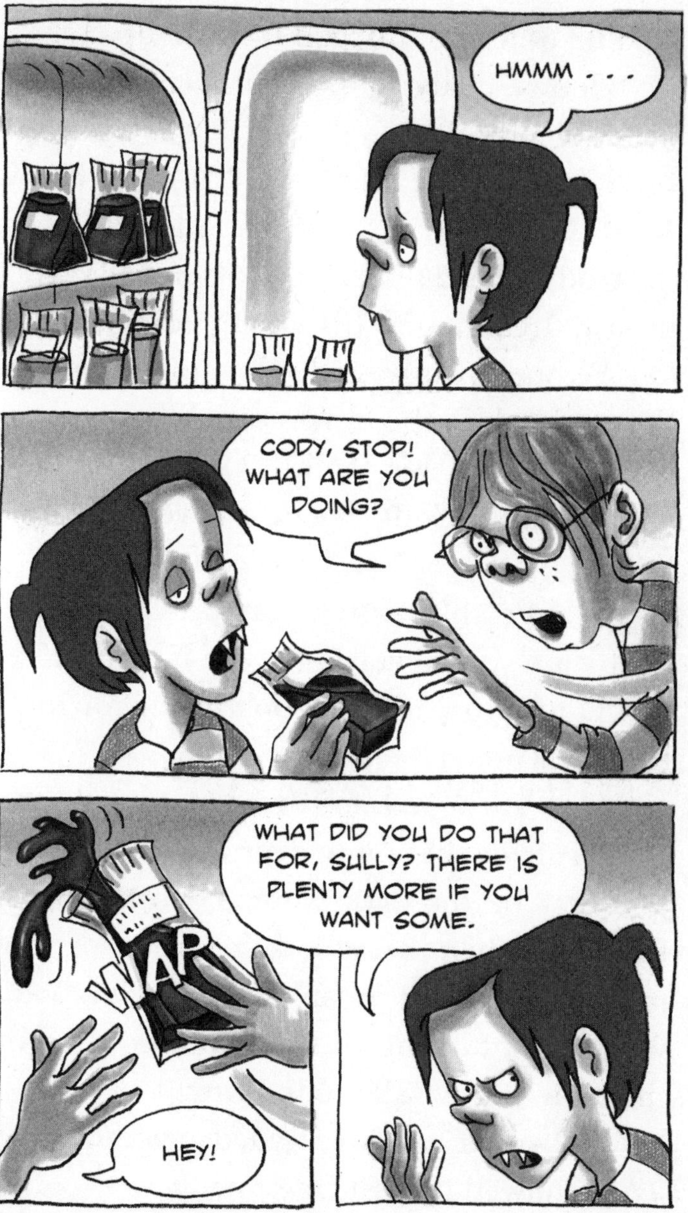
HMMM . . .
CODY, STOP! WHAT ARE YOU DOING?
WAP
HEY!
WHAT DID YOU DO THAT FOR, SULLY? THERE IS PLENTY MORE IF YOU WANT SOME.

The other boys began to wake up.

"Cody," Sully said. "You were about to drink blood!"

"No, I wasn't," he said. "It was cherry Kool-Aid."

Cody's head felt full of cotton balls. Was he still dreaming? This was too confusing.

"Wrong," Sully said. He flipped on the light. "Look in the mirror, man."

"Check out his teeth!" Carlos said. He was staring at Cody like he'd never seen him before.

"What's the matter, guys?" Cody said. "Why are you all staring at me like that?"

"Dude, you'd better look in the mirror," Ratface said.

Cody shrugged and headed over to the small mirror that hung over the sink.

Must be his eyes weren't working yet. Because when he stood in front of the mirror, his head wasn't there. His body was, but not his head. He could see straight through to the wall behind him.

The other boys crowded around him. *They* showed up just fine.

"What is this," Cody said, "some kind of trick mirror?"

Sully's jaw dropped. "It's worse than I thought," he said. "C-Cody, y-you're . . ."

"I'm what?" Cody snapped. "Tell me! Why is everyone acting this way?"

"You're becoming a vampire," Sully said.

The other boys began backing away.

Cody began to feel a sinking dread in his stomach.

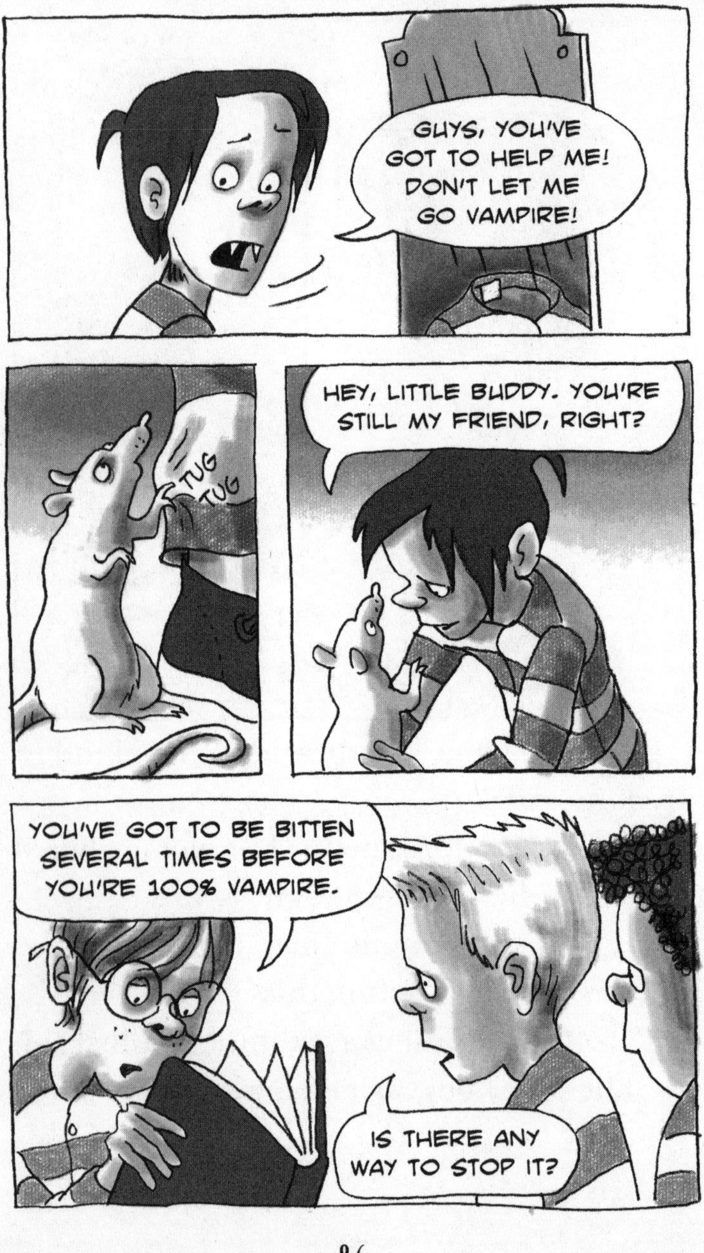
GUYS, YOU'VE GOT TO HELP ME! DON'T LET ME GO VAMPIRE!
TUG TUG
HEY, LITTLE BUDDY. YOU'RE STILL MY FRIEND, RIGHT?
YOU'VE GOT TO BE BITTEN SEVERAL TIMES BEFORE YOU'RE 100% VAMPIRE.
IS THERE ANY WAY TO STOP IT?

"'The only way to stop someone from turning into a vampire,'" Sully said, flipping through the pages of his book, "'is to get rid of the vampire who's biting them.'"

For a moment no one spoke.

"G-get rid of," Ratface stammered, "as in k-k-kill?"

Sully nodded, wide-eyed.

"I'm a thief, not a murderer!" Ratface wailed. "I'm not qualified for the job!"

Mugsy nervously twisted his uniform into knots. "You sure that's the only way?" he said. "Couldn't Cody just . . . take a course or something? Maybe swallow some aspirin?"

"You said, 'get rid of the vampire who's biting him,'" Victor said. "But who's biting Cody? It takes a vampire to make a vampire. And Farley's underground. Isn't he?"

"That's what's so weird," Sully said. "There must be another vampire at Splurch Academy who we don't know about. But who?"

CHAPTER NINE
THE MONSTER

Cody petted Rasputin and tried to think, but his mind was too jangly. He paced the floor. Farley. Vampire. The strange dreams. The bites on his neck. What could it mean? The infirmary walls spun before his eyes.

Me, a vampire?

I'm only a kid! I can't be a vampire!

"Maybe you'd better lie down, Cody," Sully said.

"I don't want to lie down!" Cody yelled. "I want to know what's going on! First all these crazy dreams, and now this. I don't get it."

"Lie down, Cody," Sully said, "and tell us about your dreams." He took a notebook and pencil from Nurse Bilgewater's desk in her office, and then sat down to listen, his legs crossed. Carlos, Mugsy, Ratface, and Victor hovered around to listen.

"Okay, Dr. Sully the shrink," Cody said. "I've been having weird dreams about Farley for a while now. They pretty much started when he was banished."

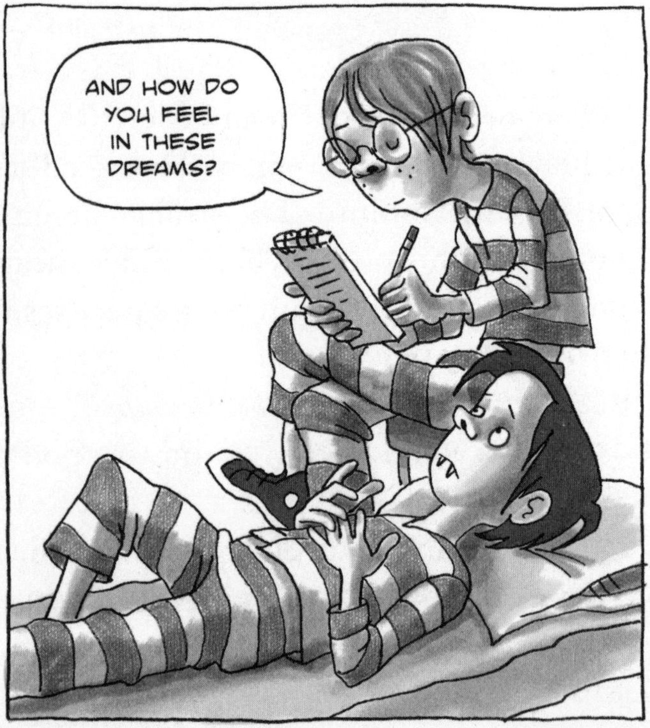
AND HOW DO YOU FEEL IN THESE DREAMS?

Cody gave him a look. "How would *you* feel if you kept having Farley dreams? They're automatic nightmares. I felt awful in them."

"Hmm." Sully scribbled in his notebook. "Proceed."

"The first time, I dreamed I was down in the crypt with Farley, only there were two of them. *Two* Farleys," Cody said. "And they were trying to use a Rebellio-Rodent Recipronator to swap my brain with a rat's. With Farley and a rat. Like a three-way swap. It doesn't make sense, I know."

"Dreams are often bewildering," Sully murmured, scribbling some notes.

"Guess so," Cody said. "The next weird dream—though I guess this has nothing to do with Farley—was when I sleepwalked out of here and ended up in the dungeons. There were bugs all over me." Cody pulled his beetle out from under his uniform. "That's where I found this guy. That's just a random accident, though. It's got nothing to do with vampires."

Sully's pencil raced across the page.

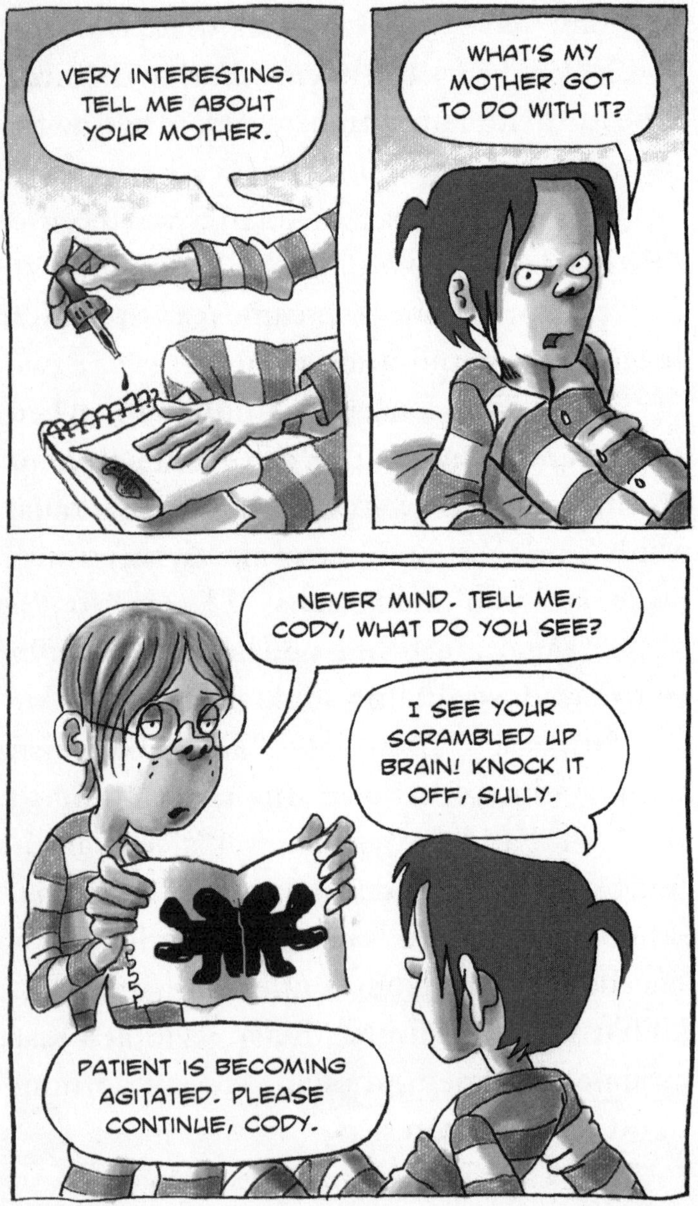
VERY INTERESTING. TELL ME ABOUT YOUR MOTHER.
WHAT'S MY MOTHER GOT TO DO WITH IT?
NEVER MIND. TELL ME, CODY, WHAT DO YOU SEE?
I SEE YOUR SCRAMBLED UP BRAIN! KNOCK IT OFF, SULLY.
PATIENT IS BECOMING AGITATED. PLEASE CONTINUE, CODY.

"So, anyway," Cody said, "last night I dreamed about a monster that whacked me on the head with some weird stick. He whacked Farley, too. This monster guy was huge, and powerful. More powerful than Farley. He kept whacking and whacking, but when he was done, Splurch Academy fell to pieces and we all went home."

The boys' eyes bugged out. "*I'll* whack you on the head if it means I can get out of here," Victor said. "Let's start doing it right now." He held up his arm, ready to strike.

"Back off!" Cody said. "The monster, he had something to do with it. It was some sort of supernatural thing, okay? And Farley. And the beetle, too. It was there. But it was only a dream, so who cares?"

"What did the monster look like?" Sully said. "Can you describe him?"

Cody tried to remember. "He had . . . a head like a crocodile. Big, snapping jaws."

Mugsy shuddered. Sully scribbled over the notebook.

"And a human body. Big and muscly."

Sully nodded. "Suspicious," he said.

"A crocodile body builder?" Victor asked.

"And a goofy costume." Cody added. "He had a skirt, and a big necklace, and something like a dish towel on his head."

"Necklace, skirt . . . crocodile. Aha!" Sully dropped his notebook. "Just as I suspected!"

The other boys looked at one another.

"What did you suspect, Sully?" Ratface asked. "That Cody's gone loopy?"

"Unlock the door, Ratface," Sully said. "We're going on a field trip to the library." And he took off running down the hall.

Mugsy groaned. "Why can't we ever take a field trip to a pizza parlor?"

The library was locked, but Ratface found the key that worked. Sully switched on one small light and went straight to a shelf of tall, dusty-looking books.

"'Ancient Mythology?'" Cody read from the spine. "So what? I don't get it."

"Check this out," Sully said, jabbing at an illustration. "Seen him recently?"

They all gathered around to look.

"That's him," Cody said. "That's the thing from my dream."

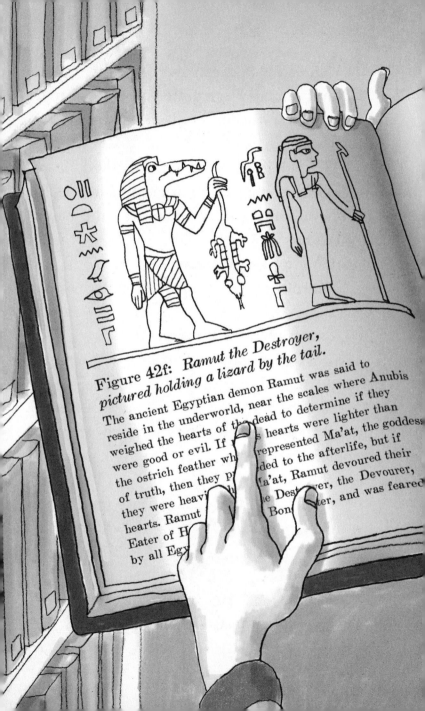

Figure 42f: *Ramut the Destroyer, pictured holding a lizard by the tail.*

The ancient Egyptian demon Ramut was said to reside in the underworld, near the scales where Anubis weighed the hearts of the dead to determine if they were good or evil. If [their] hearts were lighter than the ostrich feather wh[ich] represented Ma'at, the goddess of truth, then they p[rocee]ded to the afterlife, but if they were heavi[er tha]n [M]a'at, Ramut devoured their hearts. Ramut [was known as t]he Dest[ro]yer, the Devourer, Eater of H[earts, and the] Bon[e Crush]er, and was feared by all Egy[ptians].

"Ramut the Destroyer," Sully read. "Demon god of destruction who devoured the hearts of those doomed to wander the underworld."

"That's bad, right?" Ratface asked.

"Look at what he's got around his neck, Cody," Carlos said. "It looks like your golden bug."

Sully flipped the page.

"There it is," he said. "It's called a . . . *scarab*."

"A scary-what?" Victor said.

"Scarab," Sully repeated, glancing through the book. "An Egyptian amulet shaped like a beetle. It says it has sacred powers. Represents the sun's power to transform things."

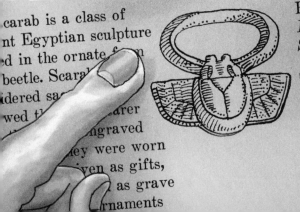

carab is a class of
nt Egyptian sculpture
d in the ornate form
beetle. Scara
idered sa
wed t   rer
              ngraved
      ey were worn
      ven as gifts,
        as grave
      rnaments

Figure 43b:
*Egyptian
Scarab amulet*

The beetle represe
cycle of life, for
sun god, Ra, rolle
across the sky an
new life and cha
disappeared only
again, so dung b
balls of dung int

Cody sat down on a library chair. He felt a little trembly. The golden beetle around his neck felt heavy, like it might choke him. What was going on? Vampires and ancient Egyptian demons and sacred bugs?

Was there something true about his dreams? Cody felt the bite marks on his neck. Something about it had to be true.

He remembered the part in the dream where his parents came and got him from the ruined Splurch Academy. Why couldn't that part of the dream be true, and all the rest of it be nonsense?

But he had a bad, goose-pimply feeling it was the other way around.

"What do we do now?" Carlos asked. "Wait for the vampire to get Cody, or the demon of destruction?"

"I'm putting my bets on the demon," Victor said. "He looks like he could kick a vampire's butt."

"Yeah, but a vampire's undead," Sully said. "That's pretty powerful, too."

"Thanks, guys," Cody said. "It's nice that I can count on you for support."

"Shh!" Ratface whispered. "What was that?"

They froze. Then they heard it, too. Footsteps. Slow, tottery footsteps like a zombie might make on its way to gobble up souls for a midnight snack.

Mmmmmmmuuuuuuuugggghhh.

A low, raspy, gravely voice. And it was coming toward them.

Mmmmmmmuuuuuuuugggghhh.

The sound came from deep in the library.

"Does that sound like a demon of destruction to you?" Carlos said. "Because it sounds like one to me."

"Who cares what it sounds like?" Cody said. "Run!"

They leaped toward the door. Just then the librarian appeared in the doorway.

"She's aiming for Cody!" Carlos yelled. "Help, guys! She's gonna get him!"

Victor scooped Cody up over his shoulder and bolted out the doorway and down the corridor, the other boys hard on his heels.

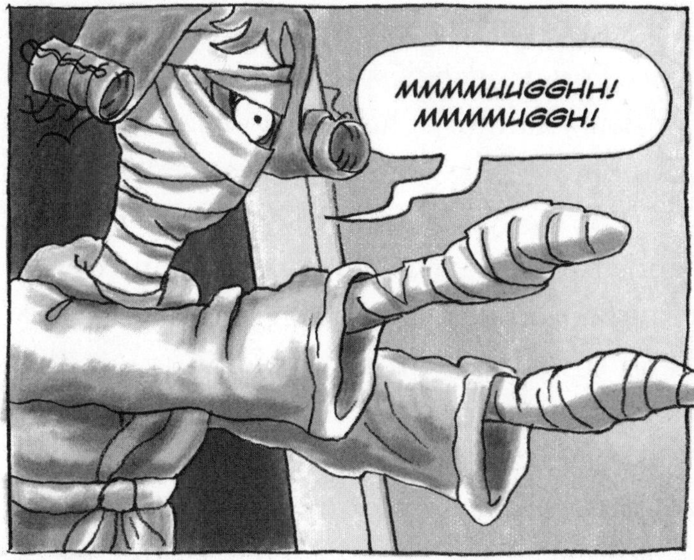
MMMMUUGGHH!
MMMMUGGH!

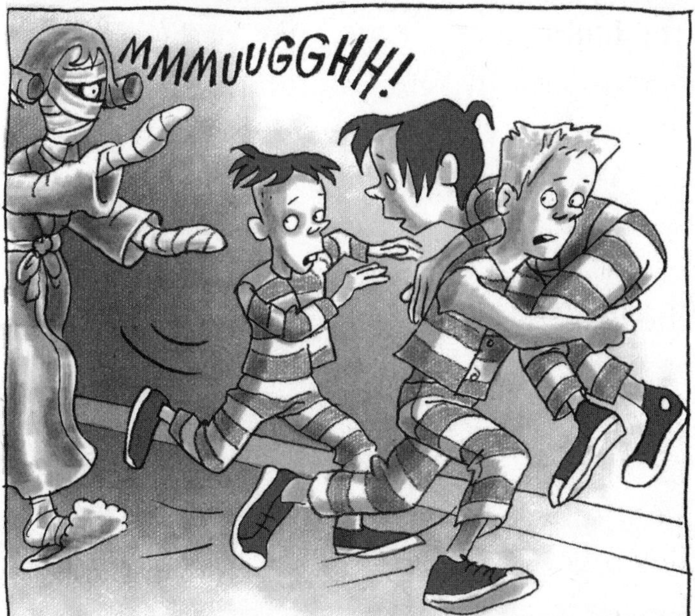
MMMUUGGHH!

Victor ran with Cody over his shoulder.

"Tough cookies, lady," Carlos yelled at the mummy. "You can't have Cody! So there!"

The boys skidded down the stairs and through the halls to the infirmary. Ratface locked the door behind them. They stood there, panting, listening for that bloodcurdling sound.

She didn't follow after them. But her moans reverberated through the pipes and heating vents of the Academy for the rest of the night.

CHAPTER TEN
THE ESCAPE

"Where's. My. CANDY!" Bilgewater roared the next morning.

Cody woke and rubbed his eyes.

She stormed through the infirmary, snatched up Mugsy with her powerful hands, and shook him till his face turned green.

"I know you're stealing my candy every night, you little maggots! May your teeth rot along with all your innards. I'll pump your stomachs to get my candy back. See if I don't!"

"How could it have been us, Nurse?" Cody said.

She strung them up by their ankles on chains hanging from the infirmary ceiling. "If you hang upside down, maybe some of my candy will dribble out your stomachs and onto the floor." She locked all the doors and left the room.

WOULD YOU SAY NURSE IS UPSET, CODY?

NAH. JUST A LITTLE OUT OF SORTS.

"Well, happy Halloween, anyway," Carlos said.

"Is today Halloween?" Ratface yipped. "Back home, I'd be bobbing for apples."

"And I'd be guzzling gallons of cider," Victor said.

"I'd have a bowl of candy corn for breakfast instead of cereal," Mugsy said. "That's sorta nutritious, right? It says 'corn' right on the package. That's a vegetable."

"No wonder your mother sent you here," Sully said.

Cody struggled to sit up in midair and unfasten his ankles. Too bad they didn't do real exercises in gym class here at Splurch. He strained and reached. No luck. If he didn't get out of here, he'd be a sitting duck when the vampire returned—whoever it was.

"Do you think she really does plan to feed us to the party guests on skewers?" Carlos said. "She did say Little Boy Shish Kebabs."

"I doubt she knows how to run a barbecue grill," Cody said.

"So much for our plans to booby-trap the

party," Victor said. "I wanted to see them freak out when the stink bombs started going off."

"Forget booby traps," Sully said. "Now how do we stop Cody from going vampire?"

Nurse Bilgewater and Miss Threadbare barged through the infirmary door, talking as though the kids weren't even there.

"I need help with the party, Beulah," Threadbare said. "Is the food ready?"

"Oh. Er . . . you betcha."

"Beulah . . . " Miss Threadbare said, tapping her toes. "You worry me."

The door opened, and Mr. Fronk and Mr. Howell appeared, each carrying a huge load of folding chairs. "Where do you want these?" Fronk said.

Miss Threadbare went to one of the infirmary windows. "Right down there," she said, pointing at the grounds below. "There's a lovely view of the party site from this window."

Fronk pulled a scrolling list from his pocket. "Get this, ladies," he said. "We've got two hundred monsters coming from all over the world,"

"Even places I've never heard of," Howell bragged, "like Moldova. And Tuvalu. And France."

"What do you mean, you've never heard of Tuvalu?" Nurse Bilgewater asked as she sampled some mixed nuts. "Everyone knows the great Tuvaluvian Vula Vulture. I hope none of those come tonight. As soon as anyone up and dies, those Vula Vultures are all over them. Won't save a bite for anyone else, no matter how nice you ask."

"Kindly don't lose our focus with talk of Vula Vultures, Beulah," Miss Threadbare said. "We have two hundred guests coming tonight. How will we manage?"

"Worry, worry, worry," Howell said. "That's all you do. You're a party pooper."

"I'm not the one who invited two hundred riffraff monsters from who knows where," Miss Threadbare squawked as they rose to leave. "I knew I should have managed the invitations. You've gotten carried away and invited all sorts of dangerous characters."

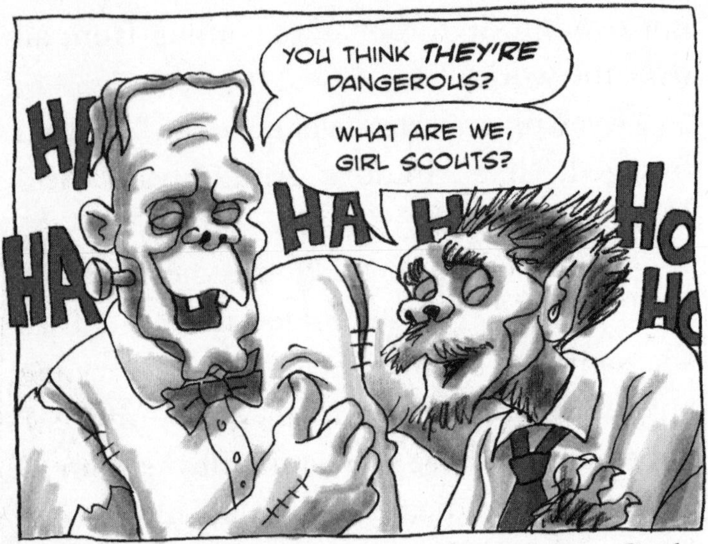
HA
HA
YOU THINK THEY'RE DANGEROUS?
WHAT ARE WE, GIRL SCOUTS?
HA
HO
HO

The teachers left the infirmary. Cody waited a minute or two to make sure they weren't coming back. "Coast is clear, guys," he said. "We've got to get to Farley's room to get our costumes and booby traps. We can smuggle our costumes back here and hide them under our cots. We can be back before they finish setting up for the party."

"I'm starving," Mugsy said. "Let's go."

Ratface stretched and struggled upright until he'd managed to unlock himself. Then he climbed up over the others, stepping on their chins and noses, and soon had everyone unlocked. One by one they fell onto their cots, rubbed their bruises, and then tiptoed out the door. Mugsy chewed on a candy bar as Cody pulled the door shut.

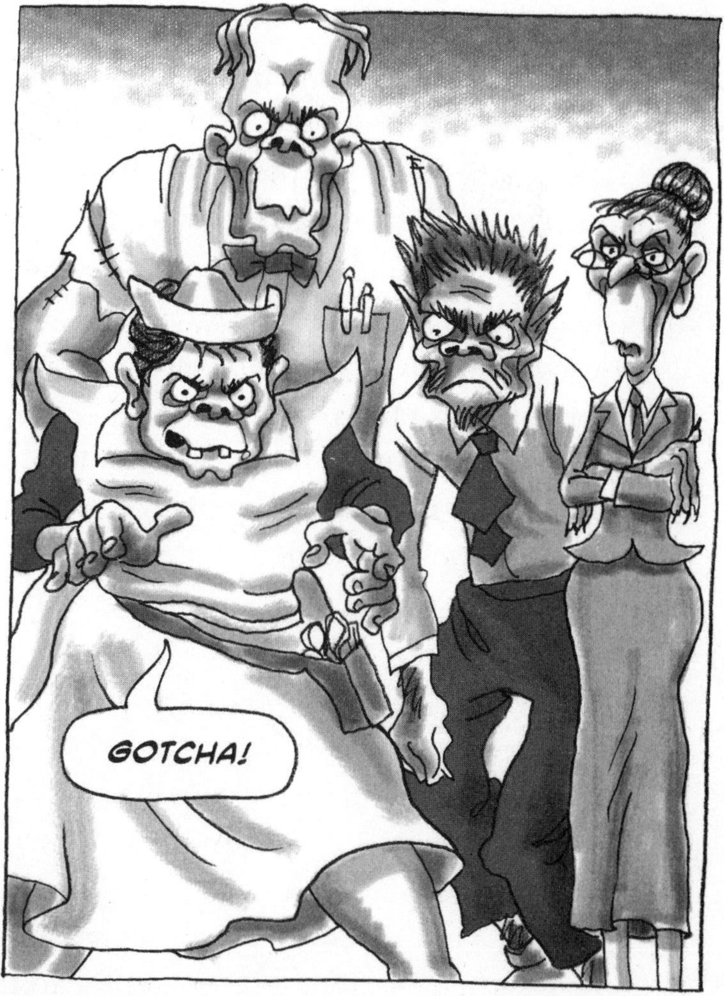
GOTCHA!

"Swiped my keys, eh?" Nurse Bilgewater hissed. "I knew the little slugs were stealing candy. How shall I punish them?"

Howell rubbed his whiskers. "Dangle them over a pit of flaming sewage?"

"Nah," Nurse Bilgewater said. "Too easy."

"Make them sleep on the tower tonight during the thunderstorm?" Fronk said.

"Yeah. In metal pajamas," Nurse Bilgewater said.

"I know," Miss Threadbare said. "Have them serve food to the party guests."

Mr. Howell elbowed Miss Threadbare. "Serve them *as* the food to the party guests, you mean."

CHAPTER ELEVEN

THE SUMMONING

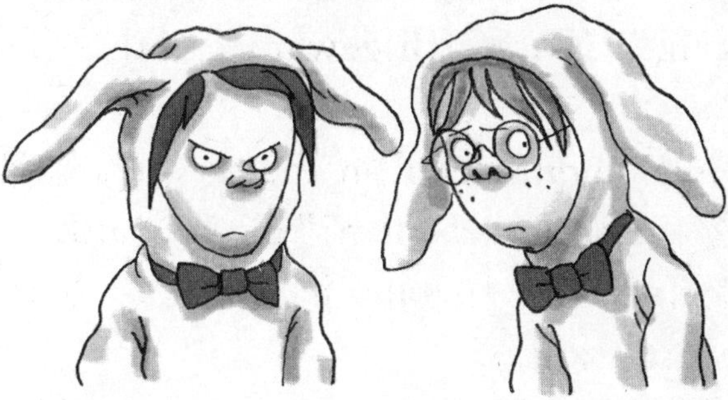

"Aren't they adorable!"

A giantess ballerina pinched Cody's cheek.

"I love bunnies," said a werewolf with an eye patch. "Soft *and* crunchy."

The boys were all dressed as pink bunny rabbits. Miss Threadbare added bow ties as a special touch. They were stuck serving party food to the ghoulish guests.

"Why would monsters bother with costumes?" Mugsy muttered.

"Do your job, rodent." Nurse Bilgewater gave Cody a kick. "Serve snacks!"

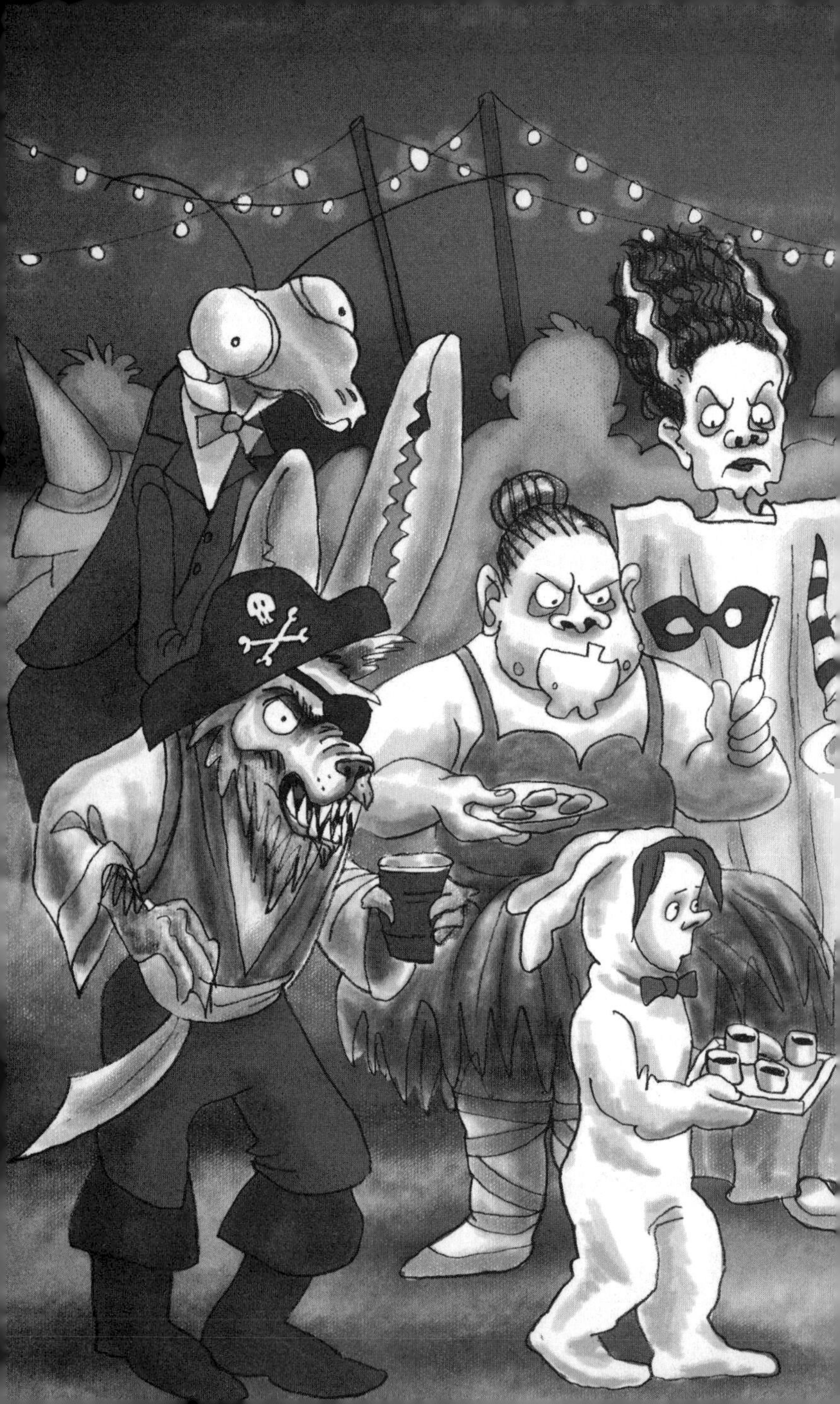

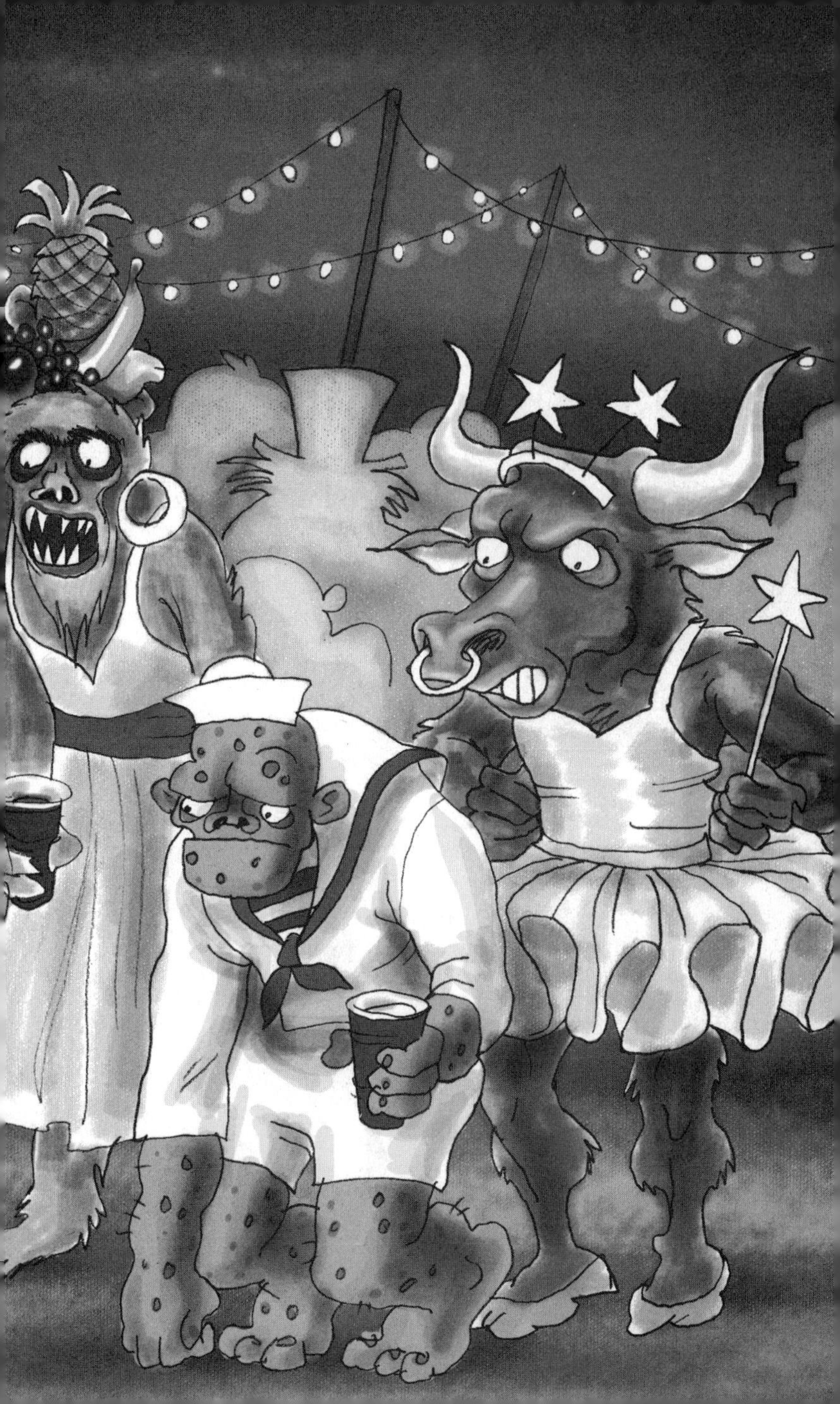

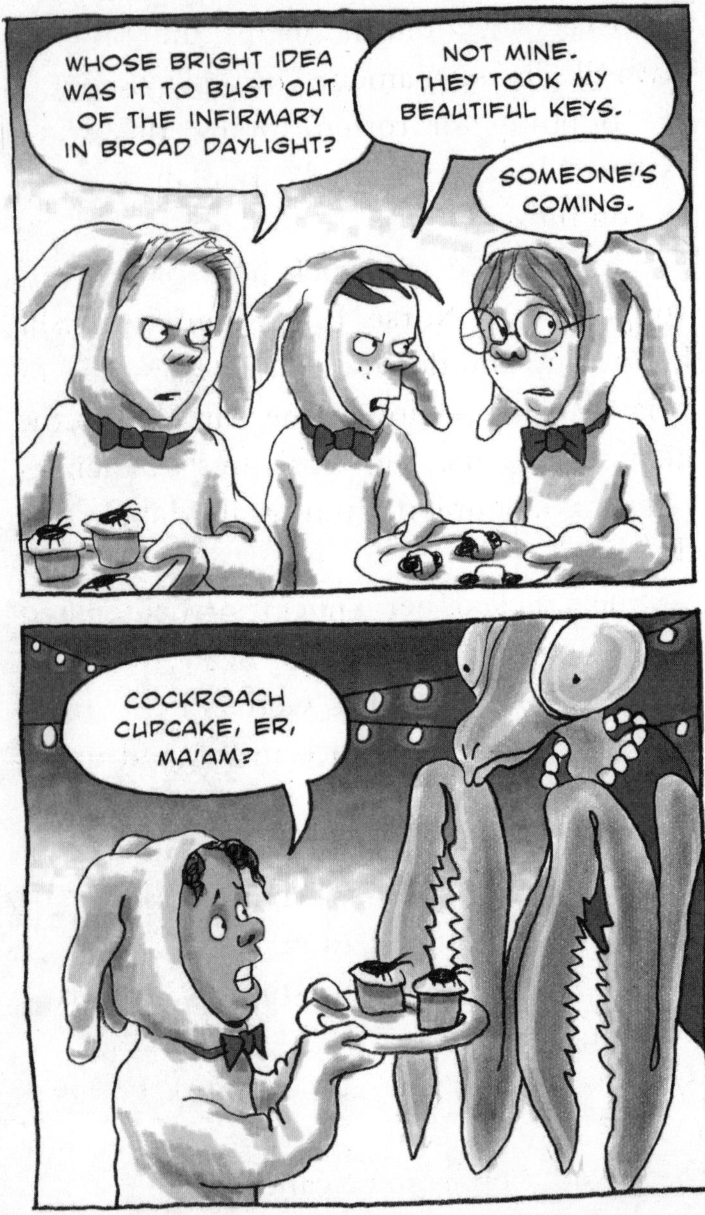
WHOSE BRIGHT IDEA WAS IT TO BUST OUT OF THE INFIRMARY IN BROAD DAYLIGHT?
NOT MINE. THEY TOOK MY BEAUTIFUL KEYS.
SOMEONE'S COMING.
COCKROACH CUPCAKE, ER, MA'AM?

"Everyone, follow me for the Bowling with Skulls tournament," Fronk yelled.

"Bobbing for rotten apples, this way," Nurse Threadbare cried. "Beulah, keep an eye on those boys."

"Figures I'd get stuck here babysitting you twerps," Nurse Bilgewater said. She hopped up and down to get a better view of what was happening at the party. "It's the gladiator fights. Big Bosephus challenges reigning champion, Immortal Mabel. Hot diggity!"

She cracked her knuckles, then glared at the boys. "What do I need to watch you for?" she said. "Come with me." Bilgewater led them back inside and up to the infirmary, then locked them inside. "You can rot here, runts. I'm off to challenge the winner of the Bosephus-Mabel fight."

Her footsteps died away.

"They can keep their stupid old party," Cody muttered.

"Wish we could get back to Farley's room," Carlos said. "Our costumes are there, and there is some candy left."

"Only the crummy stuff," Ratface said.

Just then, something clinked onto the floor, just under the door. Ratface ran over to see. "It's a key!" He picked it up and stuck it in the lock. "It works!"

"But who put it there?" Sully said.

Ratface looked up and down the hall. "I don't see anybody."

Rasputin scampered into the room and jumped up onto Cody's shoulder.

"What are we waiting for?" Carlos said. They tiptoed through the halls to Farley's room. Cody didn't see much point in it. Why put on a silly vampire suit, when he was about to *become* a vampire?

They reached Farley's room. Uncle Rastus sat in a different spot from where they'd left him. Weird.

They zipped off their bunny suits and put on their own monster costumes. Victor was an ancient Roman dude in a toga. Mugsy was a skeleton, Carlos was a Mad Hatter, Ratface was a pirate, and Sully was the Tin Man. Cody put his vampire suit on, complete with Farley's cape.

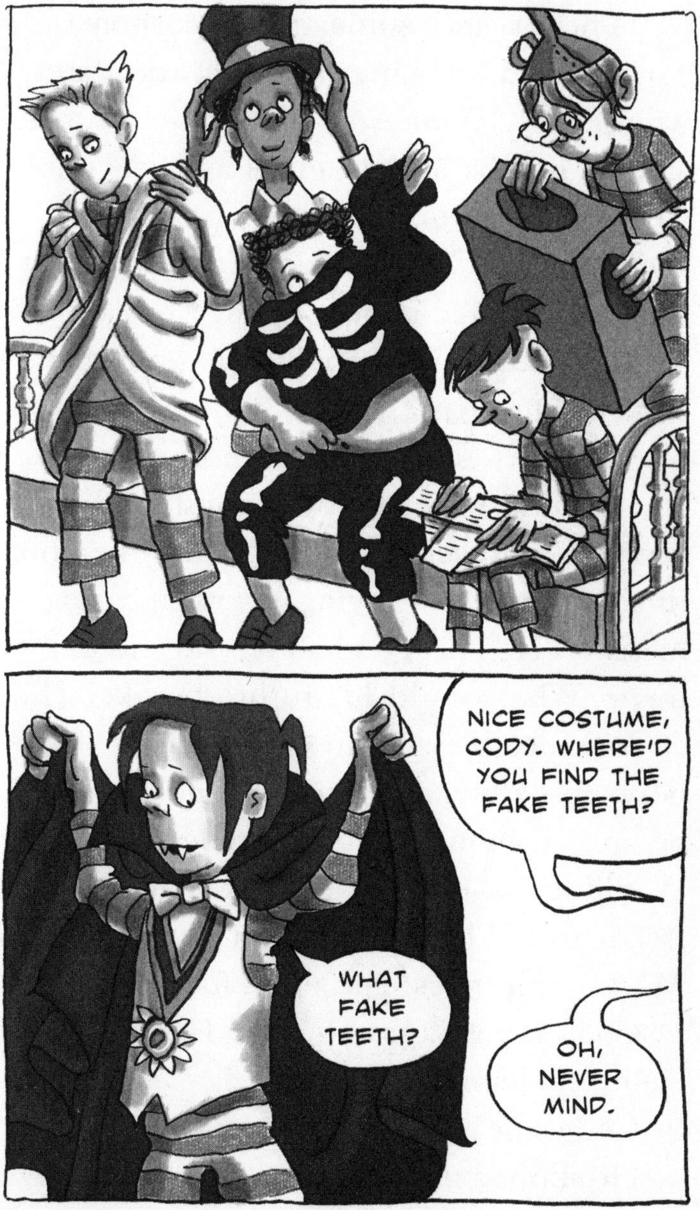
NICE COSTUME, CODY. WHERE'D YOU FIND THE FAKE TEETH?
WHAT FAKE TEETH?
OH, NEVER MIND.

"There's still some candy corn here," Mugsy said, pawing through the candy wrappings. "Ooh! And some butterscotch, and fire bombs, and the gross root beer ones. Come and get 'em!"

The other boys dived into the candy mess and started gobbling, but Cody didn't have the heart for it. He just sat on Farley's bed, feeling depressed. It was too late for his friends to save him. He knew it was. He was turning into a vampire, and he'd be a vampire forever. These might be his final moments of being a kid and not a monster. He felt too gloomy to try to enjoy them. What would his future be like? His eternal, deathless future . . . Because he'd never live a life, nor grow old and die. He'd be an evil monster for an endless eternity. Would he have to get a job here at Splurch Academy? Where else could he go? Cody Mack, vampire cafeteria boy, forever.

Cody's eyelids grew heavily. He stretched, feeling suddenly sleepy.

Cody's head drooped forward.

He slipped into a trance.

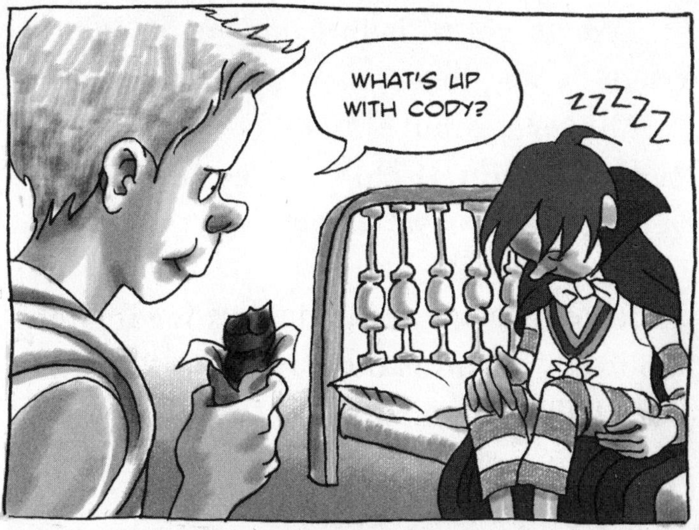
WHAT'S UP WITH CODY?
ZZZZZZ

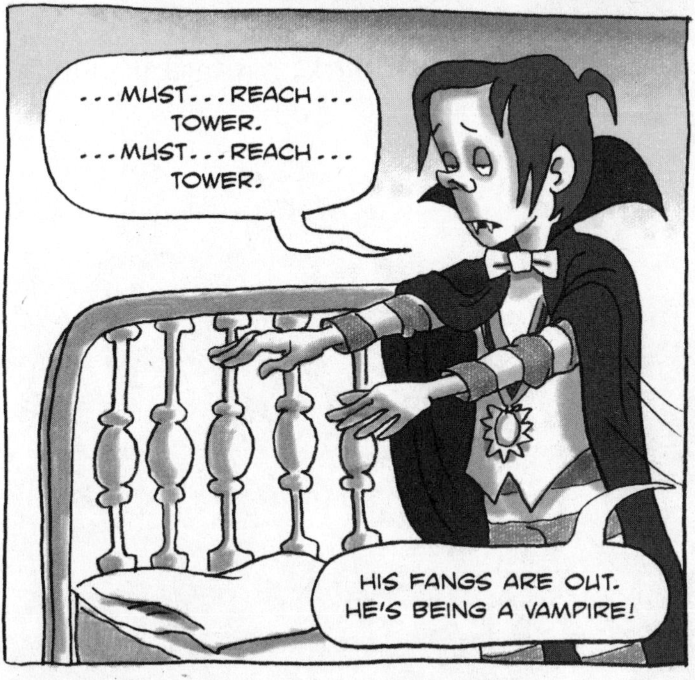
...MUST...REACH... TOWER. ...MUST...REACH... TOWER.
HIS FANGS ARE OUT. HE'S BEING A VAMPIRE!

"We've got to help Cody, guys!" Carlos cried. "Cody, man, snap out of it!"

"Never mind Cody," Sully said. "Look at the rat! He's . . . gesturing! He's *making Cody move*! C'mon, guys, we've got to follow them!"

Rasputin waved and beckoned. Cody followed, his arms outstretched. The other boys followed, terrified.

"Cody's possessed!" Ratface whispered.

They made their way up the stairs leading to the topmost tower. Outside, the sky was thick with dark, gathering clouds.

The winds whipped at their cardboard costumes as they stood there, watching the rat lead Cody on.

"Shouldn't we stop them?" Carlos said. "What if Cody gets hurt?"

Just then, Cody took the beetle out from under his clothes. It began to glow with a bright golden green light. Cody began doing weird squatty dance moves.

"Hi-ya bee-tle na-vel fluff," Cody chanted in a high voice. *"Come on, bee-tle, do your stuff!"*

The beetle's golden wings flew open.

Brrrzzzz went the wings, sounding like propeller blades on an airplane. Its glow began to pulse to the beat of Cody's chanting. Cody stomped and jumped and danced to the beat.

"Gol-den bee-tle from the past,
Do your hoo-doo, do it fast,
Big fat bee-tle, weighs a ton,
Make your ma-gic. Get it done."

Black clouds churned overhead. Thunder rumbled in the distance.

Down on the grounds, the monsters whooped and hollered at their party, unaware of the gathering storm above.

Mugsy tugged on Cody's cloak. "Cody," he cried. "Whatever you're doing, stop it!"

But Cody repeated his chant.

The sky grew thicker and darker with deadly black clouds, a whirling vortex of sinister Nature.

Cody's vampire cloak flapped in the howling wind. His vampire fangs gleamed.

Brrrzzzz went the beetle's wings.

A bolt of lightning split the sky.

It struck the tower!

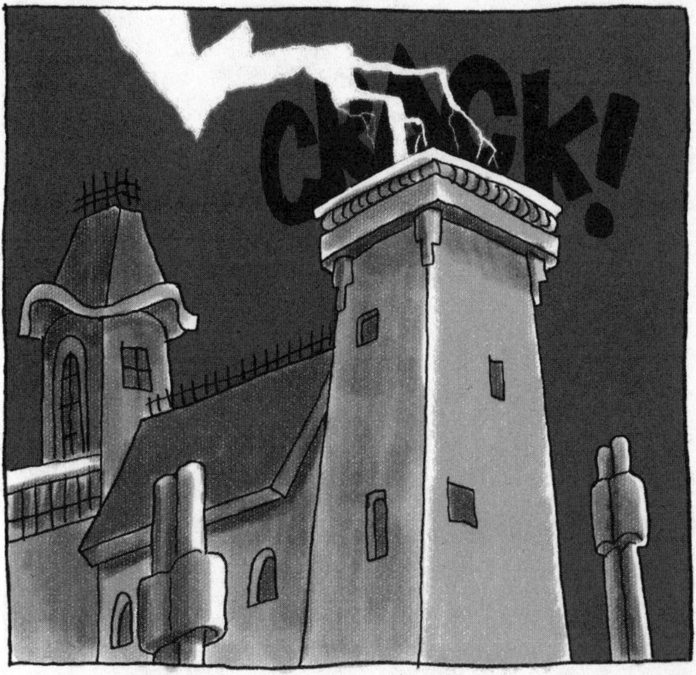
CRACK!

Cody collapsed. The glowing beetle went dark, and slipped back under Cody's shirt as he toppled to the ground.

Where the lightning struck the tower stood a monster. A huge, fearsome monster. It radiated with power.

"Yikes!" Ratface cried. He hid behind Mugsy, his knees knocking together.

"Mommy!" Mugsy yipped.

"Sully," Victor said slowly, "what . . . is . . . that?"

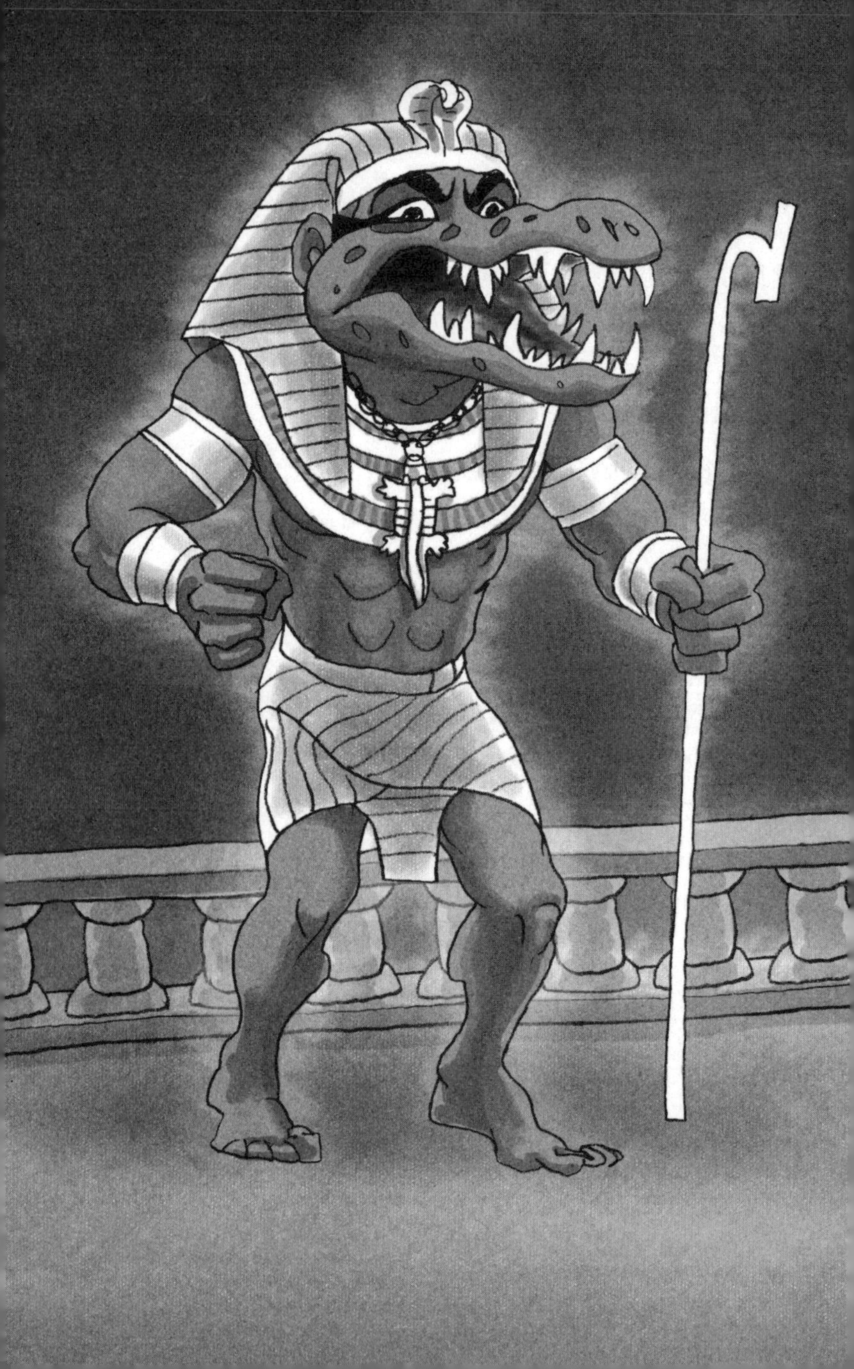

Sully looked white as a sheet. "It's Ram-m-m-mut the D-destroyer."

Victor gulped. "Thought so."

The monster took no notice of the kids. He flexed his gigantic muscles, roared, and then vaulted over the top of the tower and leaped onto the grounds below.

"What's he doing?" Mugsy cried. "Where's the crocodile guy going?"

"Never mind him," Carlos said. "What about Cody? Look at him!"

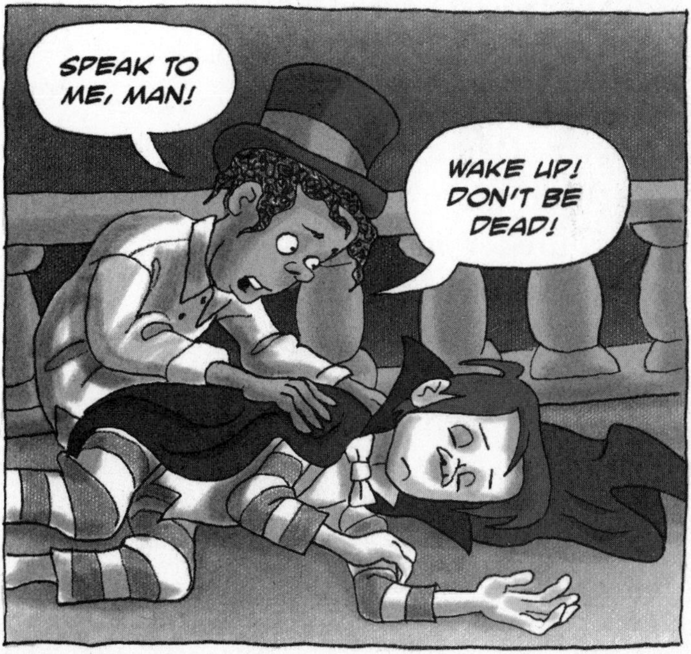
SPEAK TO ME, MAN!
WAKE UP! DON'T BE DEAD!

Cody's eyes opened slowly. He blinked. "What happened?" He looked around. "How'd I get here?"

"It was the rat that made you do it," Sully said, pointing to Rasputin. "He put you under a spell!"

Rasputin reared up on his hind legs and hissed at Sully. His little fangs shone in the gleam of a second bolt of lightning far away. Then he turned and disappeared through a gap in the tower stones.

"What do you mean, it was the rat?" Cody said. "That doesn't make sense."

"Don't you see?" Sully said. "The vampire. The sleepwalking. The beetle. The little bites. Rasputin's fangs. Haven't you figured it out? Rasputin is the vampire, Cody. *Rasputin is Farley*!"

CHAPTER TWELVE

THE PLAN

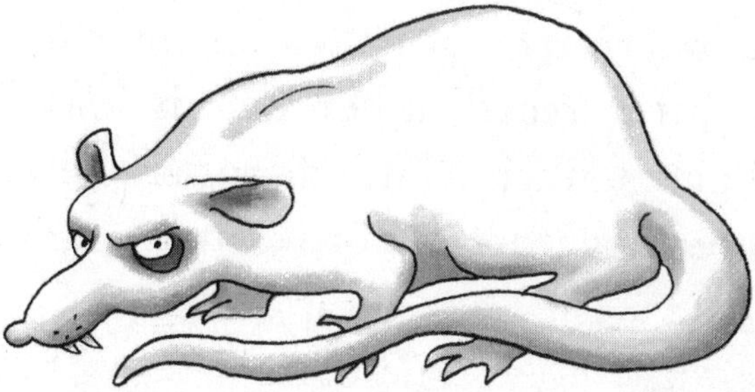

"That's impossible," Ratface said. "Rasputin's not Farley. Farley's asleep in his crypt. We saw his mother put him there."

"Then who's been biting Cody?" Sully said. "And why did Rasputin act so weird tonight?"

"The only way Rasputin could be Farley . . ." Victor began.

". . . is if they've brain-swapped," Mugsy said. "Whoa."

"A vampire rat!" Ratface said.

Cody was still in a daze. He wasn't sure which way was up. And, he was thirsty.

Mugsy waved his hands in the air. "Wait. Wait. The Recipronator plunger-thingy was destroyed. Remember? Farley dropped it and smashed it?"

"Aha," Sully said, "but think back, guys. Remember? Rasputin was on his shoulder when he dropped it. And Cody was right there next to them. They all sort of fell down in a heap together. Before it smashed."

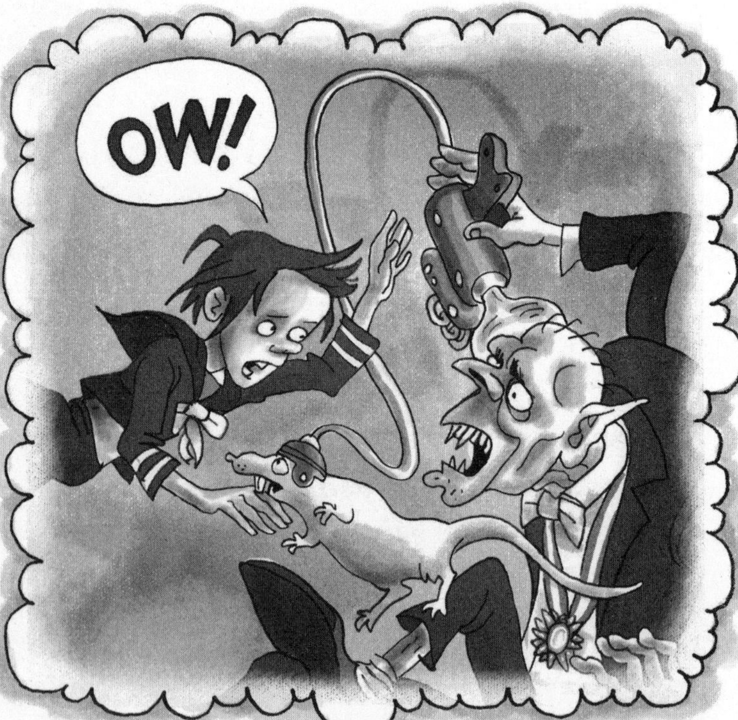
OW!

"Wasn't that when the rat bit Cody?" Carlos said. "On his hand? That bite that just won't go away?"

The boys all stared at one another. Sully started pacing around the tower in circles. The storm still raged overhead, and the monsters' shrieks and whoops almost drowned out the thunder.

"What if . . ." Sully said, "what if Farley and Rasputin brain-swapped at just that moment, while Rasputin bit Cody?"

"A three-way swap?" Victor said. "Vampire-rat-boy? That's crazy!"

"But it's the only thing that makes sense," Sully said. "Cody dreams about Farley. Cody sleepwalks and finds the bug in the basement. Maybe . . . maybe because Farley was a rat, he hung out in the basement, and found the funky bug. He discovered the bug had powers. He controlled Cody by turning him into a vampire, because Rasputin— I mean, Farley—always cuddled up under Cody's chin at night!" Sully pointed an accusing finger at Cody's neck bites. "Dude, you've been sleeping with the enemy."

"Don't forget the food!" Mugsy added, hopping up and down. "Cody wants blood because he's part vampire, and he wants cheese because he is part rat!"

Cody gradually felt his head clear. "No way, man," he said. "That's nuts. No way is Rasputin Farley. Rasputin's my *friend*."

"You didn't see him just now," Sully said. "Hissing and showing us his fangs. He's a vampire rat, all right. And he's got you under mind-control because you're turning into one of his vampire minions. We all saw him put you in a daze and bring you up here. But what I want to know is, why?"

"Um . . . what did I do while I was in a daze?" Cody said. "Besides come up here?"

"Oh, not much," Sully said, shrugging. "Only summon an ancient Egyptian demon god of wrath with your fashion necklace."

"I summoned a *what*?" Cody gasped. "Where? Who? How? Are you *sure*?"

"Hey, don't be so mean to Cody," Carlos said. "He's had a bad day."

"He'll have a worse day if Farley bites him again," Sully warned.

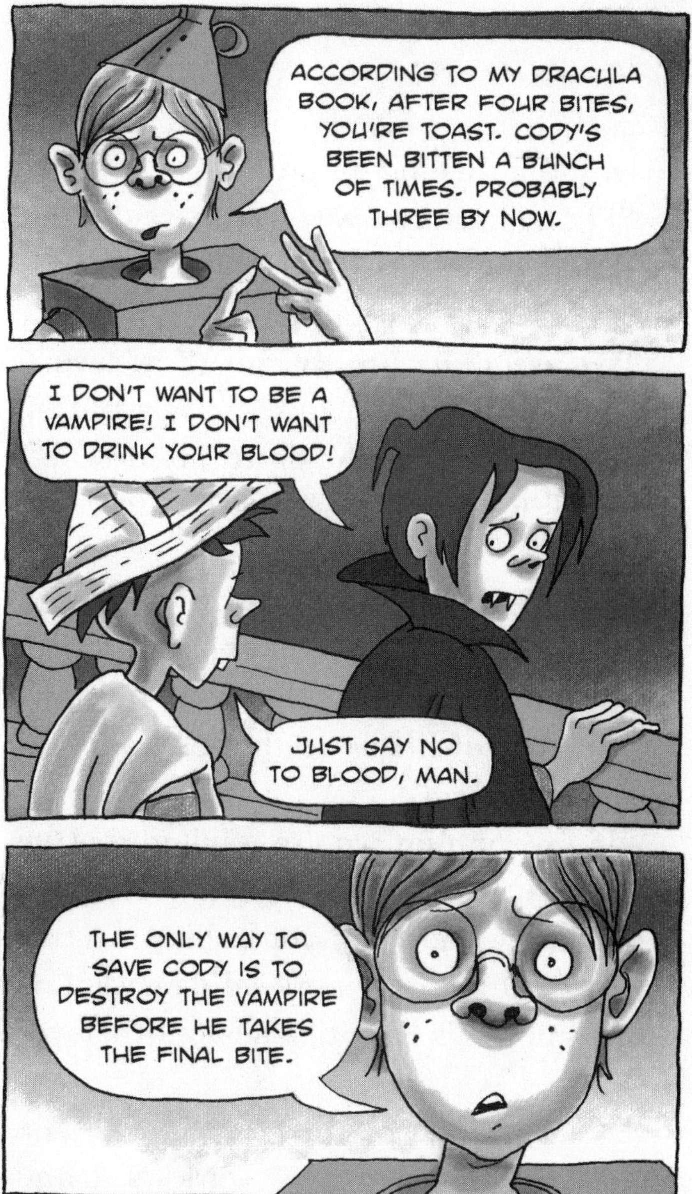
ACCORDING TO MY DRACULA BOOK, AFTER FOUR BITES, YOU'RE TOAST. CODY'S BEEN BITTEN A BUNCH OF TIMES. PROBABLY THREE BY NOW.
I DON'T WANT TO BE A VAMPIRE! I DON'T WANT TO DRINK YOUR BLOOD!
JUST SAY NO TO BLOOD, MAN.
THE ONLY WAY TO SAVE CODY IS TO DESTROY THE VAMPIRE BEFORE HE TAKES THE FINAL BITE.

"How will we ever catch Rasputin?" Victor asked. "He knows we're onto him now. He'll just hide. We'll never find one smart rat in this big dump."

"There must be a way," Sully said.

"How do you kill a vampire, anyway?" Victor asked.

"We use garlic," Sully said. "And a stake through his heart."

"There's lotsa garlic down in Griselda's kitchen," Ratface said. "Want me to go get some?"

"Let me think," Sully said.

Cody tried to think, too. It was so creepy knowing he'd been hypnotized. But, this was a matter of life or death! Being alive . . . or being *un-dead*.

"If everything you're saying is true, Sully," Cody said, "about Rasputin being Farley, and mind-controlling me, then what I want to know is, *why* did he want me summoning this Egyptian demon whatever-he-is?"

Sully snapped his fingers. "Now you're onto something. What's Farley's game?

What does he want with this demon bozo?"

"Uh, Sully," Mugsy said. "I wouldn't go calling him bozo. That Ramut guy, he looks like he could fry you with his eyeballs."

"Let's all pretend we're Farley," Sully said. "What do we want if we're Farley?"

"Let's not and say we did," Ratface said.

"Cody's life is on the line," Carlos said.

"Okay, fine," Ratface said. "If I'm Farley, I want to drink some poor kid's blood."

"If I'm Farley, I want to bust out of the underground crypt and get free," Victor said.

"If I'm Farley, I want my brain back," Mugsy said. "Or my body. Whichever."

"A-*ha*," Sully said. "But you can't do any of those things, because you're trapped in a crypt, and your brain's inside a rat, and the Recipronator is smashed. So what's the only thing that can help you now?"

They looked at one another. "A god?"

"But where is Ramut now?" Victor asked.

They all peered down over the tower railings.

The other monsters hadn't noticed the

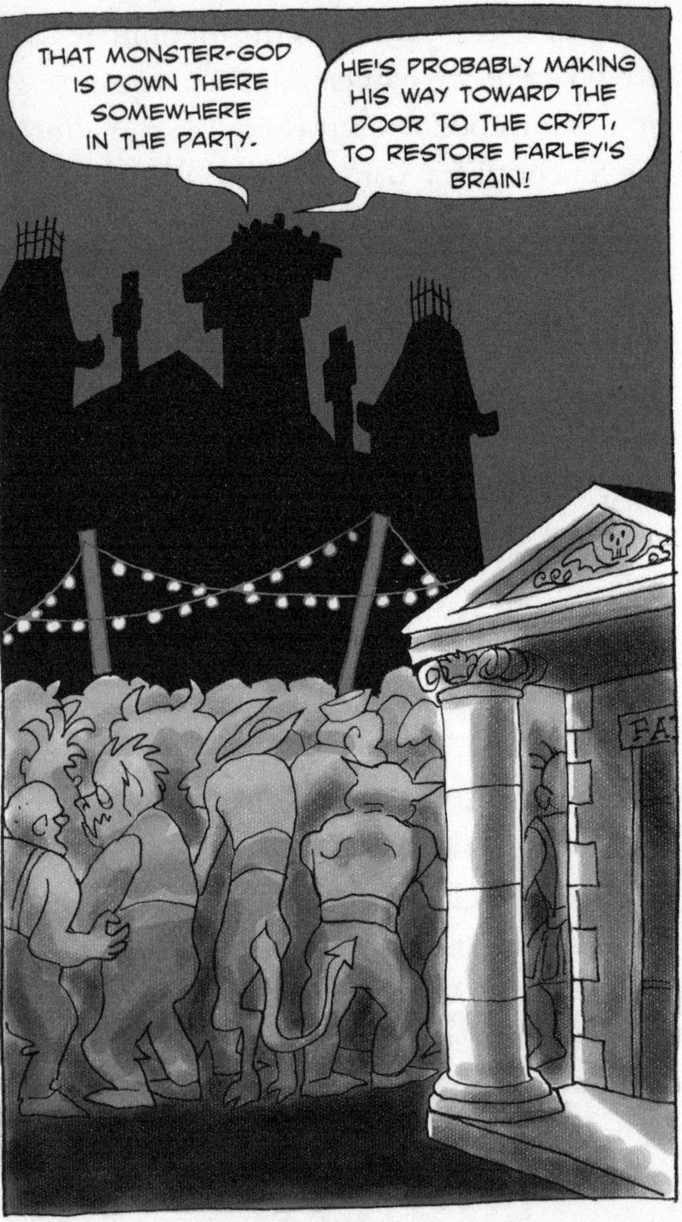
THAT MONSTER-GOD IS DOWN THERE SOMEWHERE IN THE PARTY.
HE'S PROBABLY MAKING HIS WAY TOWARD THE DOOR TO THE CRYPT, TO RESTORE FARLEY'S BRAIN!

demon. They cavorted around bonfires and ate skewers of roasted . . . something.

"There's the entrance to the Farley family crypt," Cody said. "Right in the middle of their party!"

"If the Egyptian god reaches Farley first, he'll use his god-powers to give Farley and Rasputin their brains back, and there'll be no stopping Farley then," Sully said.

"Nor will there be any way to save Cody," Carlos added.

"We've got to get to Farley's body and destroy it with garlic and stuff before Ramut finds the crypt," Carlos said.

"To the kitchens!" Ratface cried. "We haven't got a second to lose!"

They raced down the stairs and through the corridors until they reached the kitchen. Ratface threw open the cupboards.

"Garlic," Sully said. "We want garlic."

"Garlic croutons?" Mugsy aked.

"Not that," Sully said. "*Real* garlic."

"Ummm . . . what does real garlic look like?" Victor asked.

"Well, I'll bring these, too," Mugsy said.

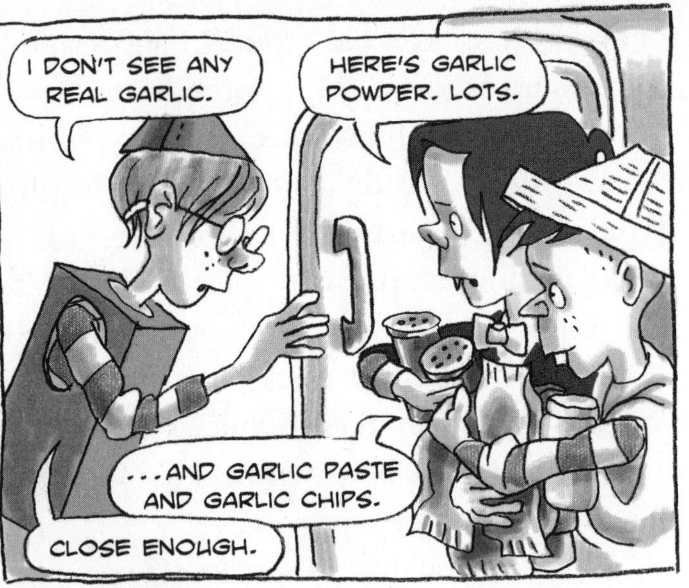
I DON'T SEE ANY REAL GARLIC.
HERE'S GARLIC POWDER. LOTS.
...AND GARLIC PASTE AND GARLIC CHIPS.
CLOSE ENOUGH.

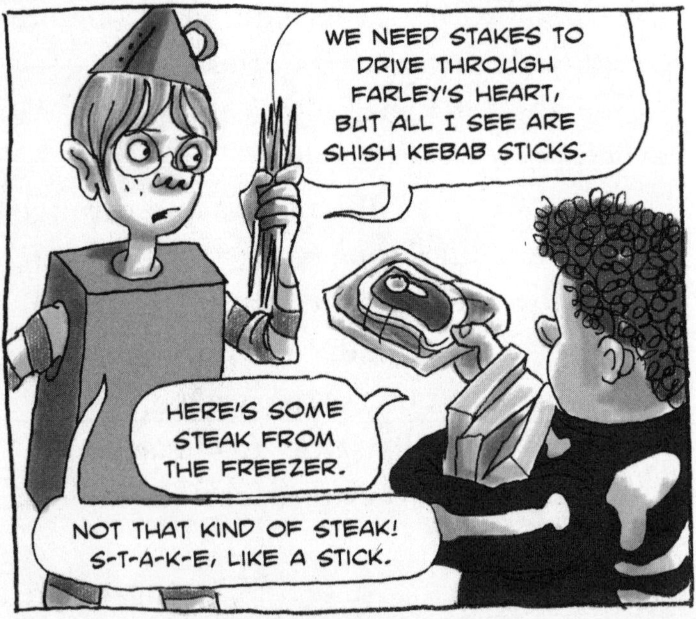
WE NEED STAKES TO DRIVE THROUGH FARLEY'S HEART, BUT ALL I SEE ARE SHISH KEBAB STICKS.
HERE'S SOME STEAK FROM THE FREEZER.
NOT THAT KIND OF STEAK! S-T-A-K-E, LIKE A STICK.

"They're hard as rocks. Could be a weapon in a pinch."

Ratface tugged on Cody's vampire cape. "Um, Cody," he said, "we're not really going out there, are we? Out into the middle of the Halloween party?"

"It's the only way to reach Farley's crypt," Cody said.

"But they'll eat us!" Ratface wailed.

"No, they won't," Sully said. "We look like monsters in our costumes."

"Um, yeah, right," Ratface said.

YOU DON'T HAVE TO GO, RATFACE. ANY OF YOU. YOU CAN STAY HERE WHERE IT'S SAFE. I'LL GO BY MYSELF. THIS IS MY PROBLEM TO SOLVE, NOT YOURS.

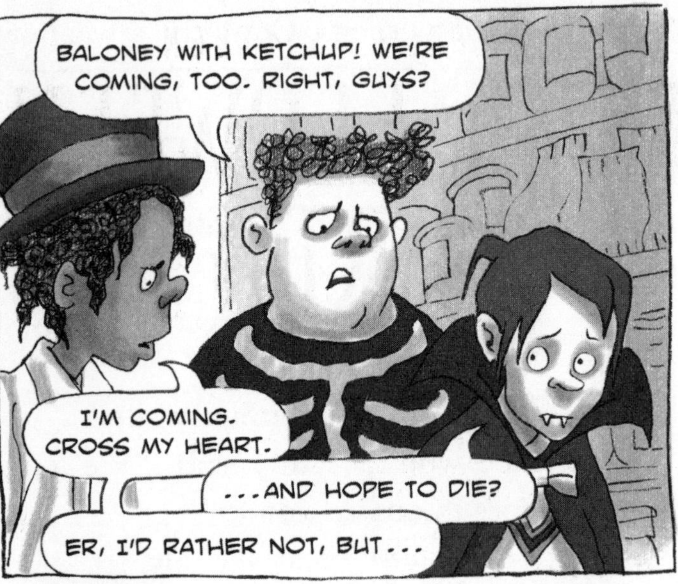
BALONEY WITH KETCHUP! WE'RE COMING, TOO. RIGHT, GUYS?
I'M COMING. CROSS MY HEART.
...AND HOPE TO DIE?
ER, I'D RATHER NOT, BUT...

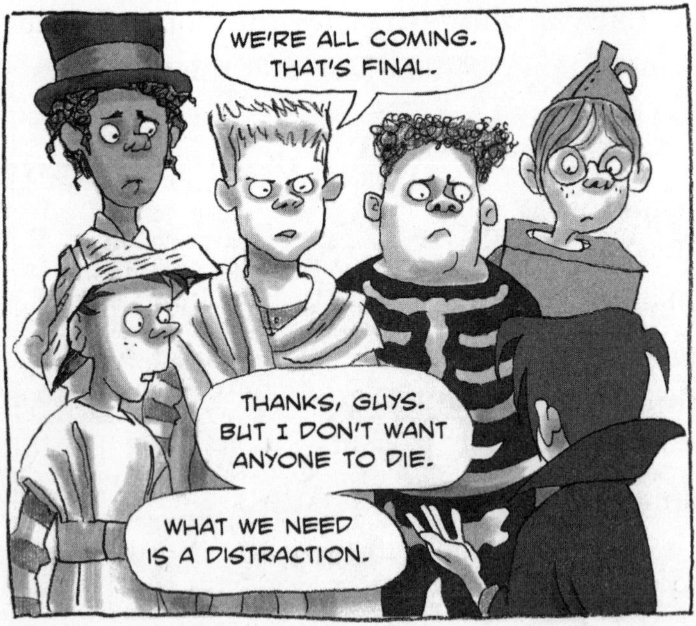
WE'RE ALL COMING. THAT'S FINAL.
THANKS, GUYS. BUT I DON'T WANT ANYONE TO DIE.
WHAT WE NEED IS A DISTRACTION.

CHAPTER THIRTEEN

THE HALLOWEEN PARTY

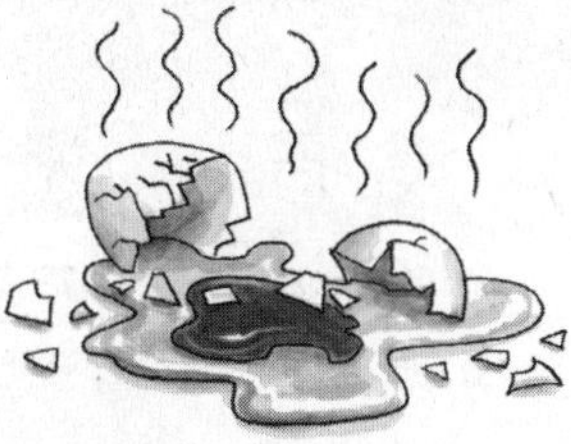

Back in the infirmary, they opened the windows and looked down at the monsters' party.

"What are they doing?" Mugsy whispered.

"It looks like some of them are playing Twister," Carlos said, pressing his face against the glass. "The squid-looking thing is winning."

"It's time to launch our attack," Cody announced.

"Been nice knowing you all," Victor said. "Let's get moving."

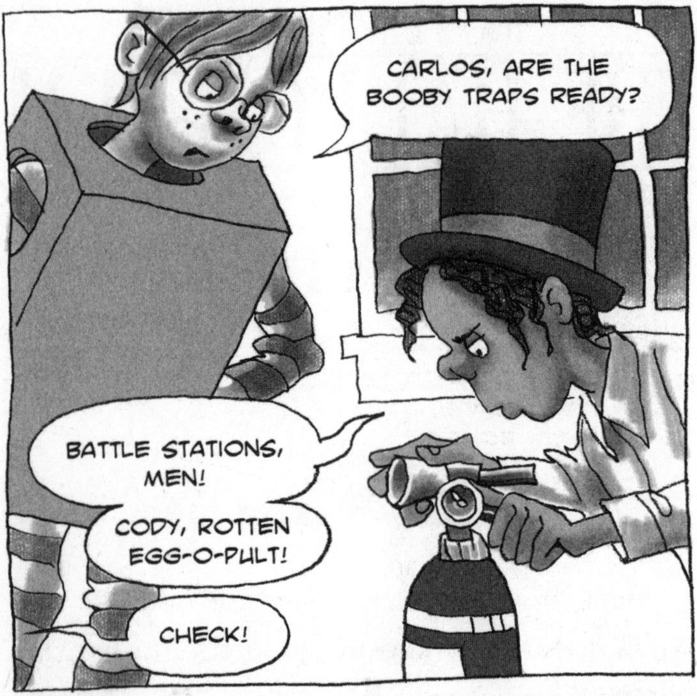
CARLOS, ARE THE BOOBY TRAPS READY?
BATTLE STATIONS, MEN!
CODY, ROTTEN EGG-O-PULT!
CHECK!

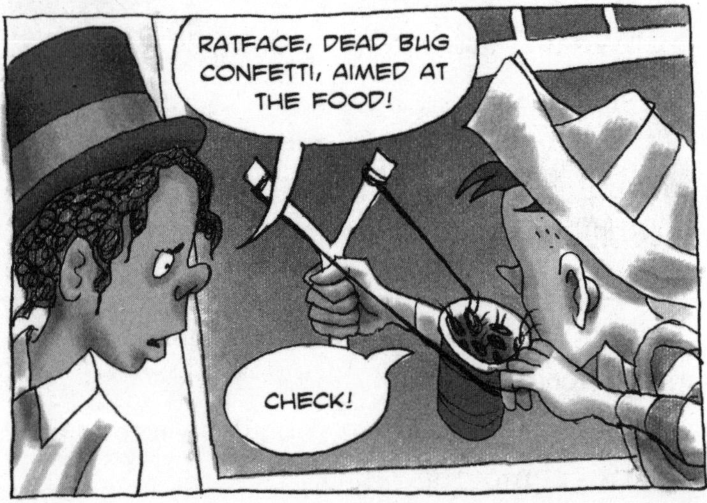
RATFACE, DEAD BUG CONFETTI, AIMED AT THE FOOD!
CHECK!

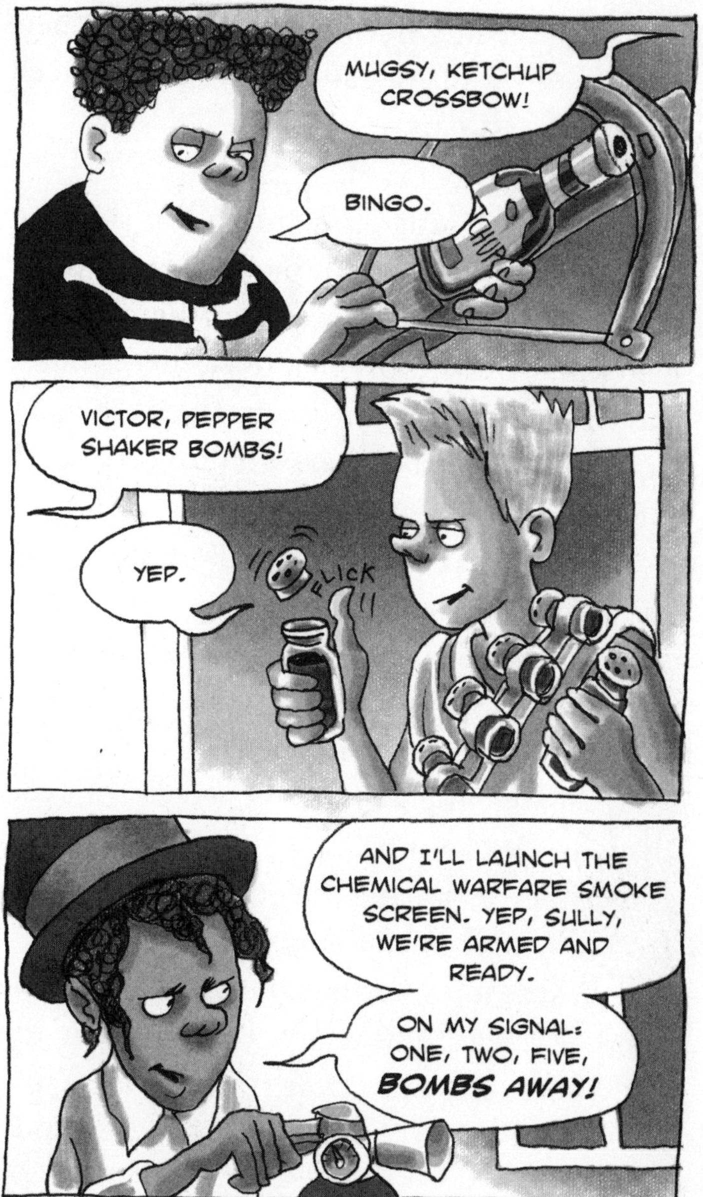
MUGSY, KETCHUP CROSSBOW!
BINGO.
VICTOR, PEPPER SHAKER BOMBS!
YEP.
FLICK
AND I'LL LAUNCH THE CHEMICAL WARFARE SMOKE SCREEN. YEP, SULLY, WE'RE ARMED AND READY.
ON MY SIGNAL: ONE, TWO, FIVE, BOMBS AWAY!

For a second nothing happened. Then shrieks and wails began ringing out all over the monsters' party.

"Run!" Cody cried.

The boys skidded into the hall and out the doors, then bolted onto the dark grounds.

Rotten-egg stink reached their noses. Ketchup squirts, pepper dust, dead bugs, and fire extinguisher foam filled the air. Cody hoped the monsters wouldn't see them through the booby-trap haze.

"Hey! What are those kids doing here? Get 'em!" bellowed a voice.

"Run! Run!" Cody gasped. They clutched their flimsy costumes and sprinted for the safety of Farley's tomb.

A loathsome, growling voice pierced the pandemonium. "I smell children, Bilgewater," it said. "You said you were fresh out. Lemme at 'em!"

"Tasty, juicy, crunchy children," came another voice. "The feisty ones squirm in the belly for a long time after you swallow 'em."

"There's the tomb, up ahead," Cody whispered.

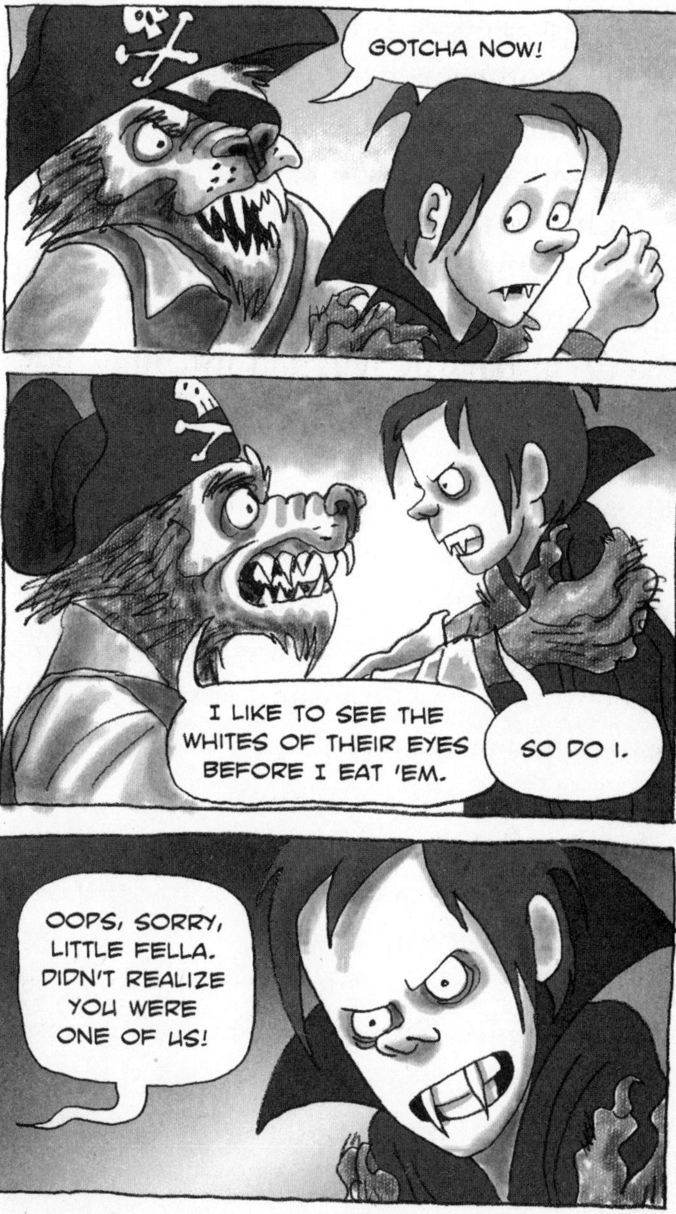
GOTCHA NOW!
I LIKE TO SEE THE WHITES OF THEIR EYES BEFORE I EAT 'EM.
SO DO I.
OOPS, SORRY, LITTLE FELLA. DIDN'T REALIZE YOU WERE ONE OF US!

Cody stumbled backward toward the crypt. His fangs were still sharp, and he still wanted to bite something. He snarled at any monsters he could see, then shook his head to try to shake off the vampire spell. He turned, hurried on, and leaped into the opening of the crypt. Down, down, down the dark stairs he fell, and the other boys tumbled after.

CHAPTER FOURTEEN
THE CRYPT

Cody was sore all over from his fall.

It was cold in the crypt, and dark. The noise and shrieks from the party aboveground faded. The cold, dark dust of the crypt muted the noise. It smelled like emptiness and decay and death.

It smelled like home for a vampire.

Cody almost liked it. He shuddered.

He couldn't see much except the walls of a narrow passageway leading somewhere he sure didn't want to go.

A bat fluttered by his face and up the stairway.

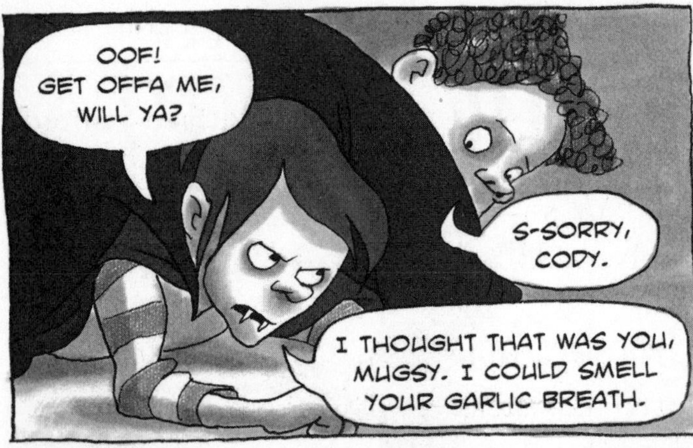
OOF!
GET OFFA ME,
WILL YA?
S-SORRY,
CODY.
I THOUGHT THAT WAS YOU,
MUGSY. I COULD SMELL
YOUR GARLIC BREATH.

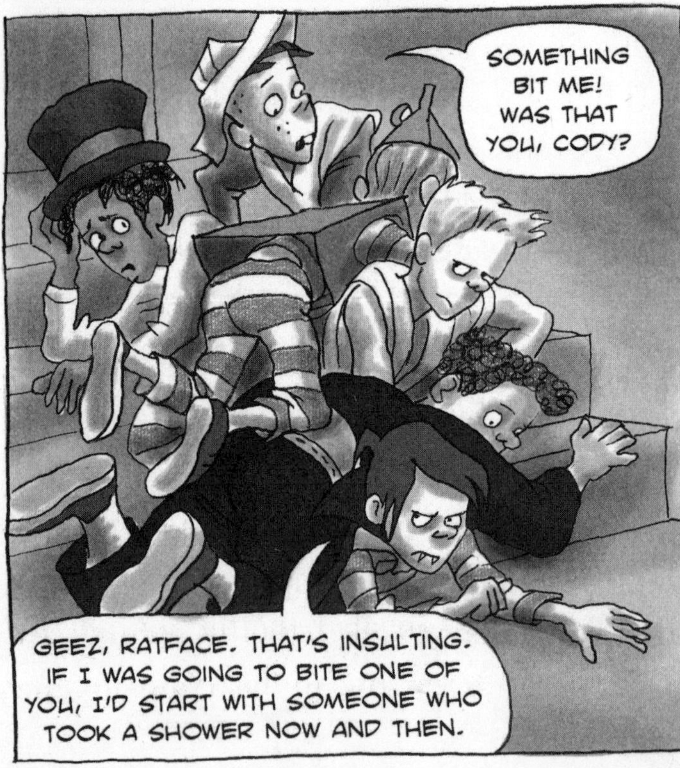
SOMETHING
BIT ME!
WAS THAT
YOU, CODY?
GEEZ, RATFACE. THAT'S INSULTING.
IF I WAS GOING TO BITE ONE OF
YOU, I'D START WITH SOMEONE WHO
TOOK A SHOWER NOW AND THEN.

"Nothing bit you," Sully said. "You landed on a rat skeleton."

"That's it. I'm done," Ratface panted. "Get me outta here."

"Not so fast," Carlos said. "We've got a job to do, and we're not leaving till it's done."

"That's right," Mugsy said. "We've got garlic and steak, and we know how to use them."

There was a pause.

They all looked at one another.

"Well, go ahead, Cody," Victor said, giving Cody's shoulders a shove. "You first. You're vampire now. This should feel like home to you."

Cody took a deep breath and stepped forward. *Crunch* went his sneakers on the little bones and leaves that lined the floor. A rough wooden door blocked the entryway to the crypt itself. He took another deep breath and pushed it open.

The hinges squealed loudly enough to wake the dead. The boys jumped.

Then, one by one, they went inside.

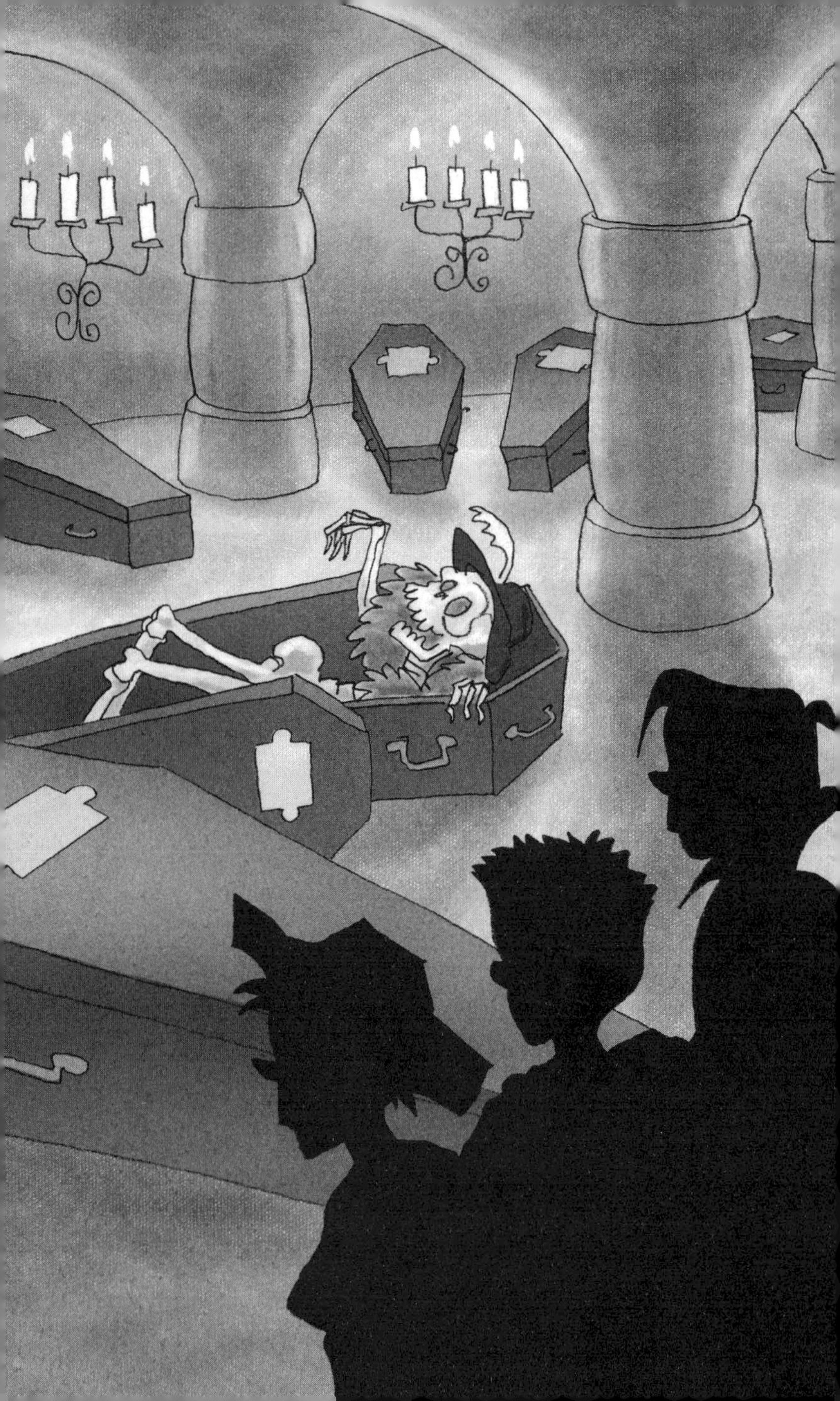

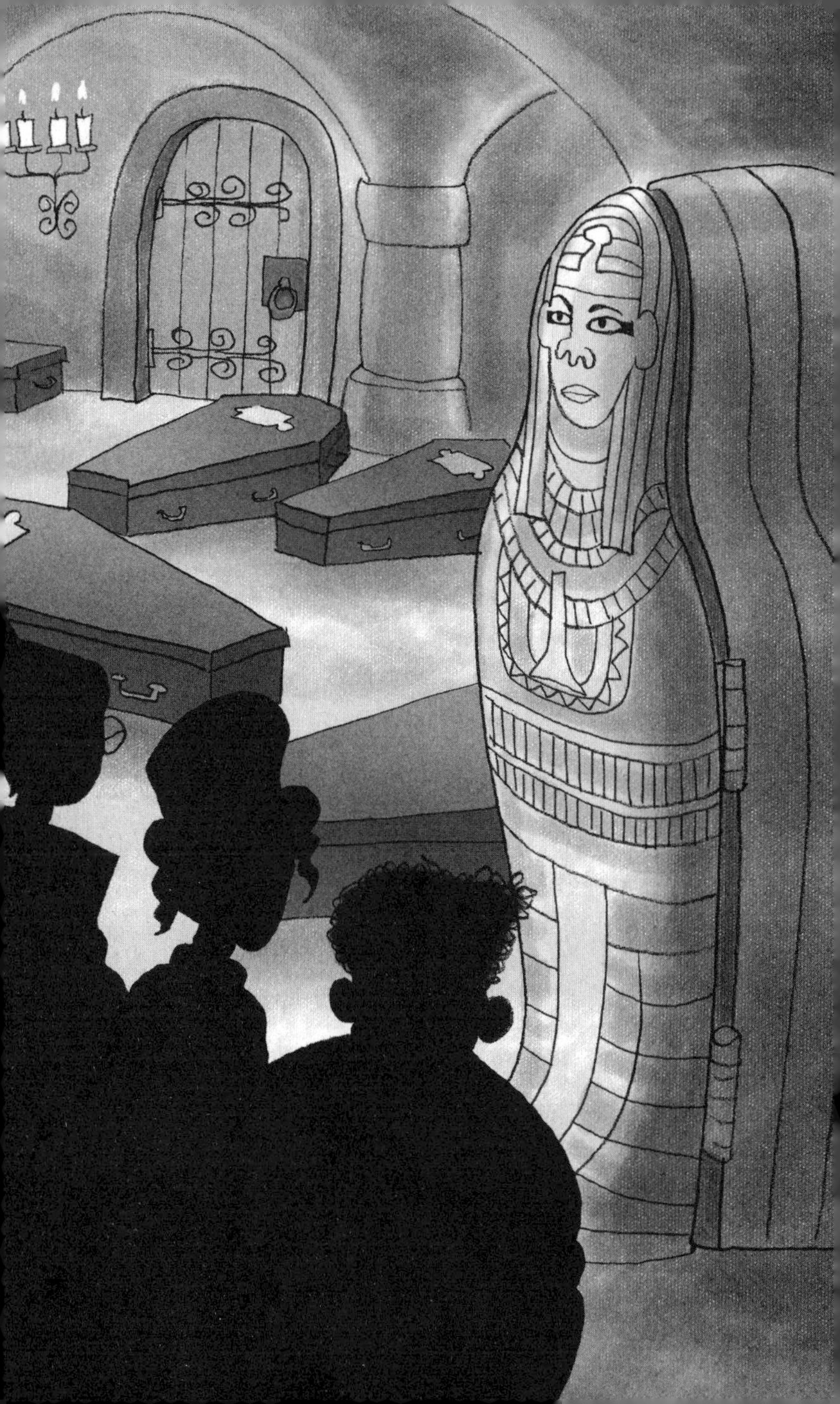

Dim, flickering light from torches on the walls moved like probing fingers across their faces, while sheets of cobwebs stirred in the air currents made by the boys' breathing.

Everywhere they looked they saw dead people. Not the people themselves. Caskets lay everywhere. A tall, ancient mummy case lay propped against one wall. A skeleton draped in the remains of a fur coat reclined in one open coffin.

"It's Uncle Rastus!" Carlos yipped.

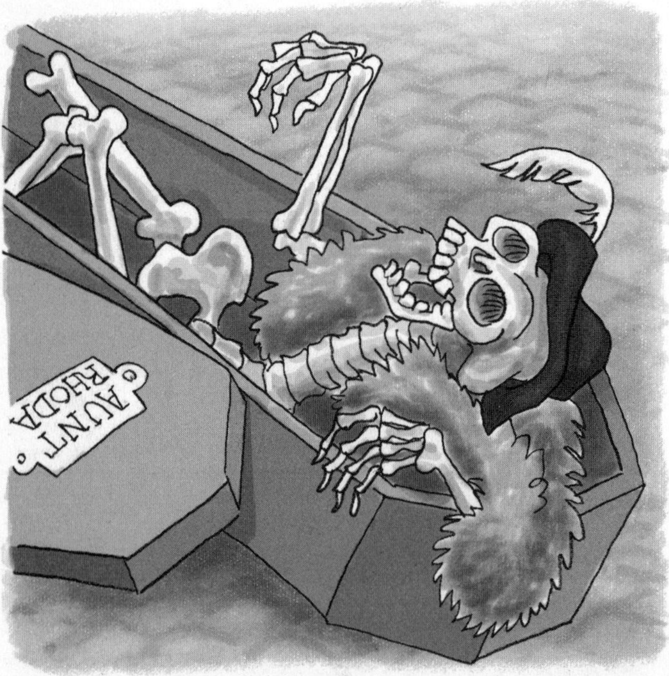
AUNT RHODA

"Nope," Sully said, reading the name plate. "It's his wife, Farley's Aunt Rhoda."

"Okay, well, the sightseeing's been great, but we've got work to do," Cody said. "Get your garlic ready. Where's Farley?"

"Isn't it obvious?" Sully pointed a shaking finger.

There, against the far wall of the crypt, sat a coffin that looked newer than the others, though that wasn't saying a lot. Cody grabbed a torch for a closer look.

ARCHIBALD FARLEY, it read. HEADMASTER AND GENIUS.

"Even when he's dead he's got a big ego," Mugsy said.

And next to it lay a *rat-sized coffin*. RASPUTIN, ALTER EGO AND SIDEKICK, it said.

"See?" Sully said. "What did I tell you? Rasputin and Farley are one."

"Hey, guys," Ratface said, "lookit this."

Just a short way off stood a brand-new coffin, medium sized. A piece of masking tape obscured the label.

Ratface peeled it off.

CODY MACK
FORMER
ENEMY

Cody felt his mouth water, his armpits sweat, his knees shake, and his eyes roll back in his head. Thirsty. Thirsty. If only he weren't so thirsty, he could think straight. But where could he get a drink? There was Carlos, right beside him, his neck within easy reach . . .

"Snap out of it!" Sully yelled. "Wake up, Cody! Don't go over to the dark side." He shoved Cody away from Carlos so he toppled onto the floor. Cody landed on his tailbone with a painful crack.

"We've got to stay focused and get the job done," Sully said. "Who knows? Any minute now, the Destroyer may figure out we're down here. Now, somebody's got to open up Farley's coffin.

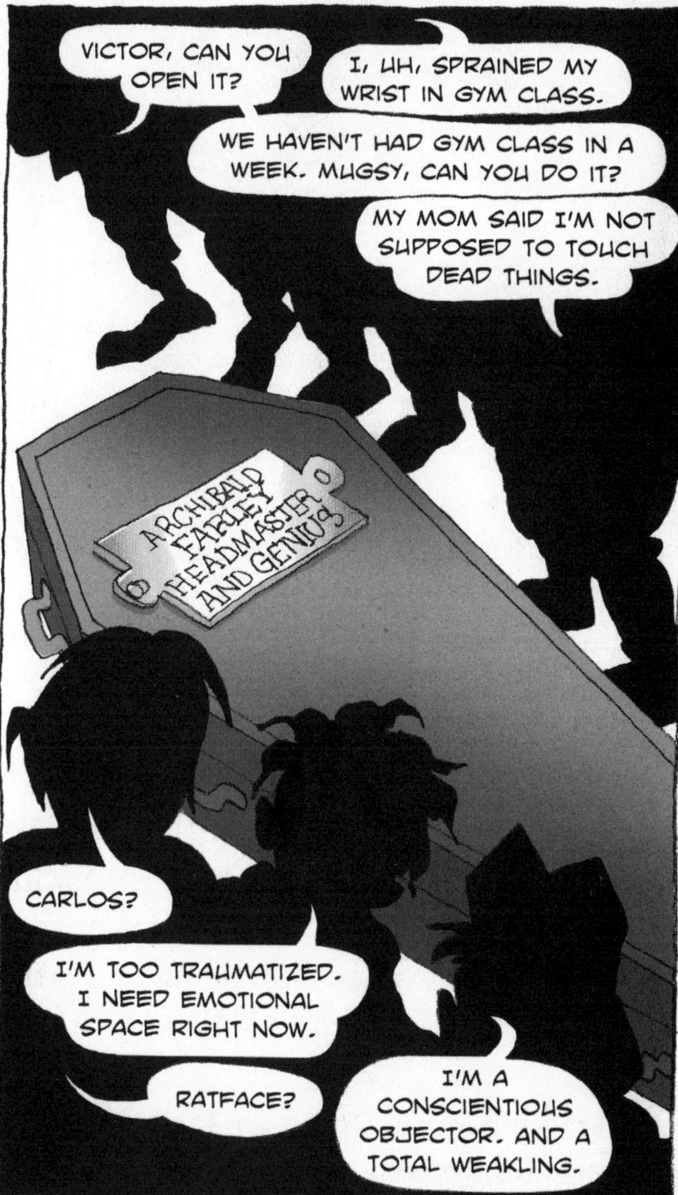
VICTOR, CAN YOU OPEN IT?
I, UH, SPRAINED MY WRIST IN GYM CLASS.
WE HAVEN'T HAD GYM CLASS IN A WEEK. MUGSY, CAN YOU DO IT?
MY MOM SAID I'M NOT SUPPOSED TO TOUCH DEAD THINGS.
ARCHIBALD FARLEY HEADMASTER AND GENIUS
CARLOS?
I'M TOO TRAUMATIZED. I NEED EMOTIONAL SPACE RIGHT NOW.
RATFACE?
I'M A CONSCIENTIOUS OBJECTOR. AND A TOTAL WEAKLING.

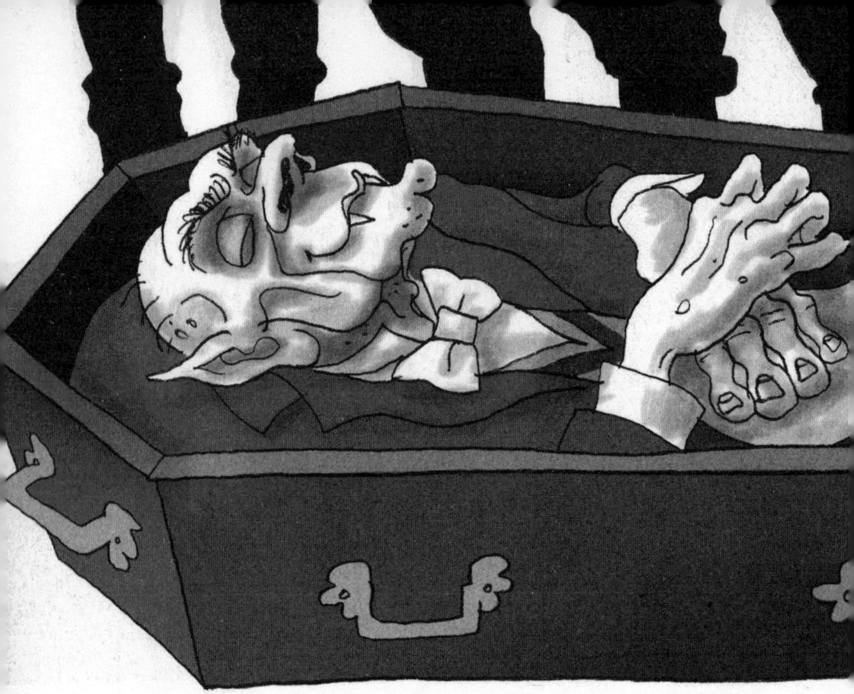

They all looked at Cody.

"All right, all right," Cody said. "I guess this is my problem, anyway."

Cody's heart pounded in his ribs. *At least I still have a beating heart*, he thought. *I'm not un-dead yet*.

He gripped the sides of the coffin. He took a deep breath. Candlelight played over the placard saying HEADMASTER AND GENIUS.

Headmaster and lying, evil, stinking, rotten, foul, treacherous . . .

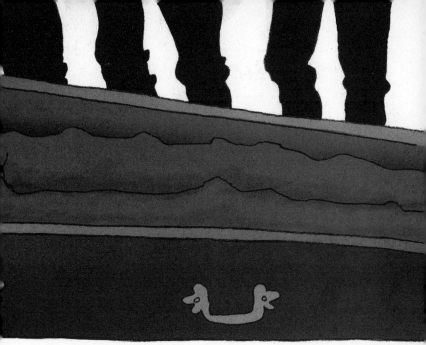

He heaved the lid open.

He didn't dare look, until . . .

"It's him," Mugsy whispered. "Farley."

"I can see right up his nostrils," Ratface said. "It's just like old times."

Cody opened his eyes. There, below him, lay the cold, waxy form of Archibald Farley, headmaster of Splurch Academy for Disruptive Boys.

Cody realized he was breathing hard, like he'd just run a marathon. He turned to Sully. It was all so creepy, being down here, looking at Farley's body like this. He wasn't sure what to do next. "Now what?"

"Now it's time to garlic him to death," Sully said.

"Are we really actually supposed to kill him?" Carlos asked.

"Think of it as saving Cody," Sully said. "And ridding the world of a dangerous vampire . . . and crummy headmaster. Everyone, get out your garlic weapons."

"Mugsy's eaten all of it," Ratface said.

"Not *all* of it." Mugsy said. "There's lots of chips left."

"Who's got the garlic paste?" Sully said.

Once they got over how gross it was to be touching an almost-dead body, they got right into their work. They squirted garlic paste in his nostrils, ears, and eye sockets. They shook garlic powder over every inch of him. They scattered garlic chips all over the paste and the powder. They smeared garlic goo over every surface of his face and hands, even yanking down his socks and sliming it over his hairy ankles.

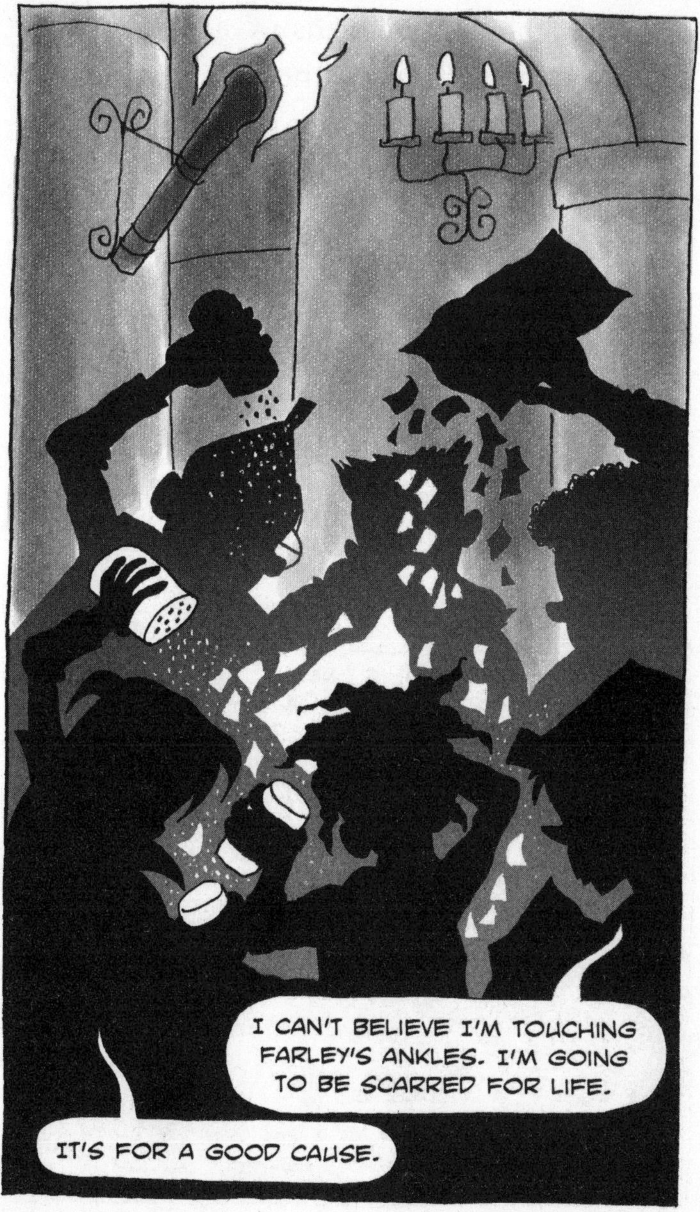
I CAN'T BELIEVE I'M TOUCHING FARLEY'S ANKLES. I'M GOING TO BE SCARRED FOR LIFE.
IT'S FOR A GOOD CAUSE.

They shook their cans of garlic powder out all over him until he was covered in little garlic powder mountains. His hair was so full of garlic powder, he looked like he was wearing a yellow powdered wig.

"I used to like garlic bread," Carlos said, "but if I survive tonight, I don't ever want to eat another bite of garlic as long as I live."

"Pee-yew!" Victor said. "This place stinks!"

"Garlic is naturally pungent," Sully began, but Ratface pointed an accusing finger at Mugsy.

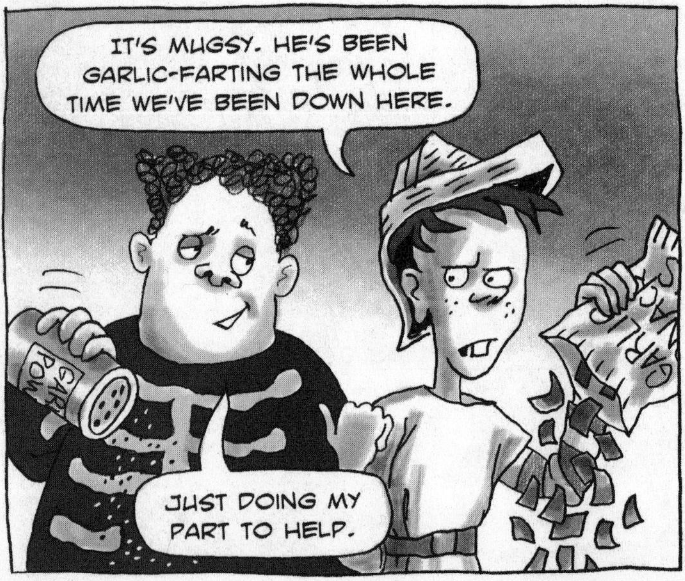
IT'S MUGSY. HE'S BEEN GARLIC-FARTING THE WHOLE TIME WE'VE BEEN DOWN HERE.
JUST DOING MY PART TO HELP.

"All right, men," Sully said, passing out shish kebab sticks. "Time to be brave. If we're going to save Cody, we've got to drive stakes through Farley's heart."

"I'm a kid, not a psychopath," Ratface said. "I'm too young and innocent for this kind of thing."

"Hooey," Carlos said. "C'mon, Ratface, help us out."

"How do you know these teensy little stakes will do the job?" Victor said. "They're the size of Pick-Up Sticks."

"All we can do is hope. Stakes ready?"

The boys nodded grimly. Except Cody, he felt like he was going to puke. All that garlic was making him light-headed. The bite wounds on his hand and neck throbbed with sharp pain.

"I can't do it, Sully," Cody whispered. "I can't explain it. I just can't."

"It's probably because Farley's partly controlling you," Sully said. "We'll do it for you. Now, everyone. One . . . two . . . three . . ."

They heard a sound. A scuffle. Maybe a

mouse. Or a bat. Probably nothing.

But the hair on the back of Cody's neck rose. Did he dare look?

Gggrrrowwwwl.

CHAPTER FIFTEEN

THE AWAKENING

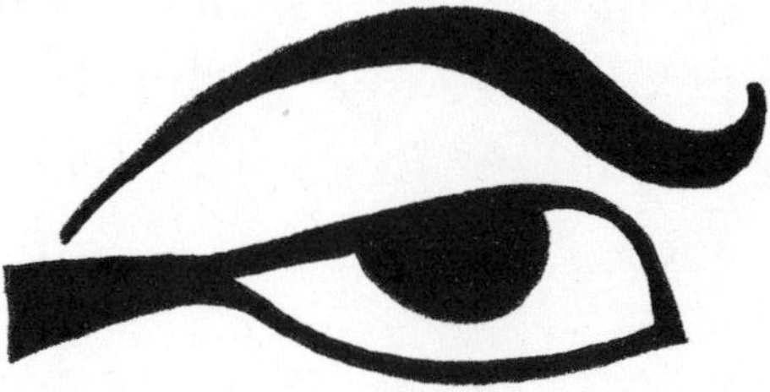

They didn't need to look. They could feel the pulsating aura of power.

It was Ramut the Destroyer, stepping out from behind a sarcophagus.

He'd gotten there first. And he wasn't going to let them finish Farley off. Had he been waiting for Cody all along?

Cody ran and stood between the other boys and the demon. The boys scrambled back as far as they could. They huddled, smooshed against a wall, and waited for those crocodile jaws to chomp down on them.

But they never chomped.

Ramut went straight to Farley's corpse and held his hand over him. There was a strong smell, like sizzling garlic sautéing in a pan, and Farley's body rose straight up from the coffin. It was as if Ramut were a magician doing a levitating trick. Farley was stiff as a poker, dead as a shish kebab stick, still covered all over in a sticky, tacky crust of garlic yuck.

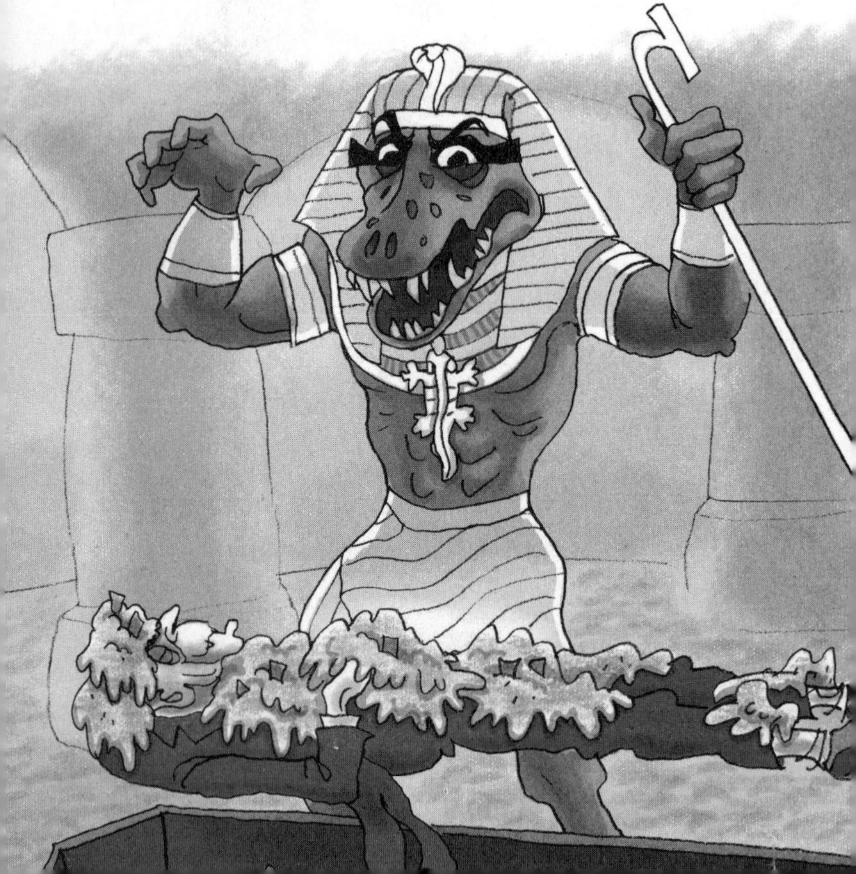

There was a scuttling sound on the ground. A live rat made its way through the jungle of rat skeletons and junk on the floor.

RASPUTIN!

YOU DIRTY RAT...

The rat scampered up to Ramut. As he tried to climb up on to the demon's foot there was a hot, hissing sound.

"Hope he burned his paws real good," Cody whispered to Sully.

"It's not the rat's fault that Farley brain-swapped him," Sully whispered back.

"I don't care."

"What's he doing now?"

The rat was bowing to Ramut, over and over, his little front paws held high above his head. Ramut bent over and held out his open hand to Rasputin, who cautiously climbed onto it. No sparks this time. Ramut placed Rasputin on top of Farley's head. Then he pointed his staff at Cody.

A beam of arcing, fizzing light zapped straight from Ramut's hand to Cody's

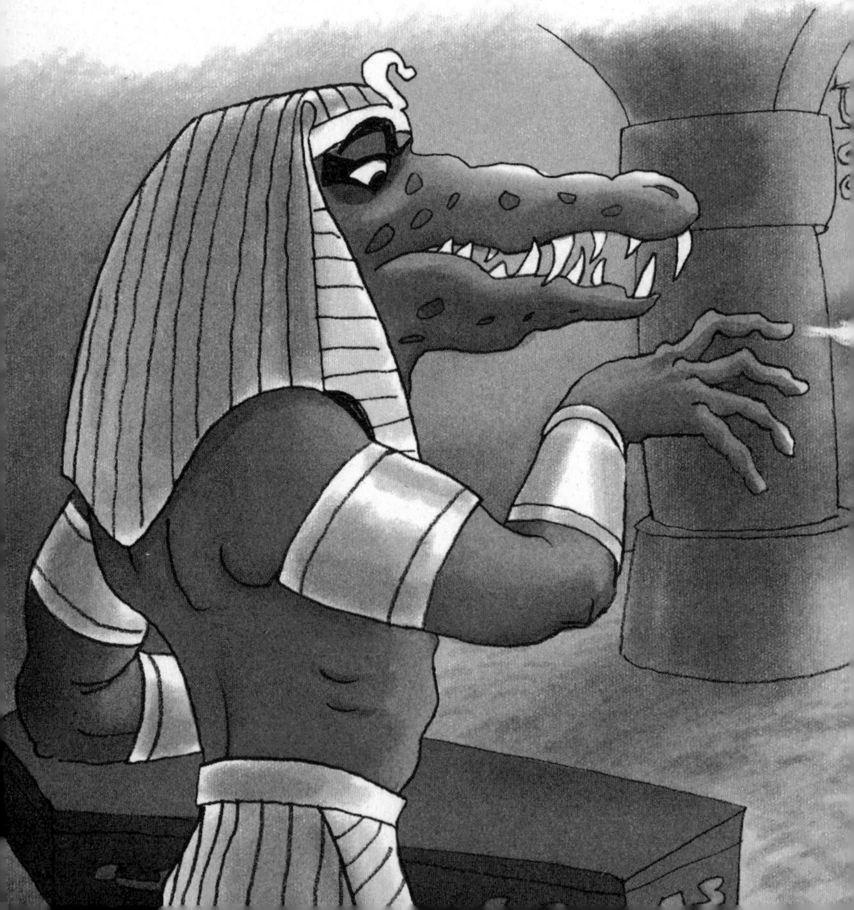

chest, and reeled Cody forward like a tractor beam. Cody kicked and swung his arms, but it did no good. The Destroyer pulled him closer, until they stood in a cozy little triangle together—Ramut, Farley's body with Rasputin on top, and Cody.

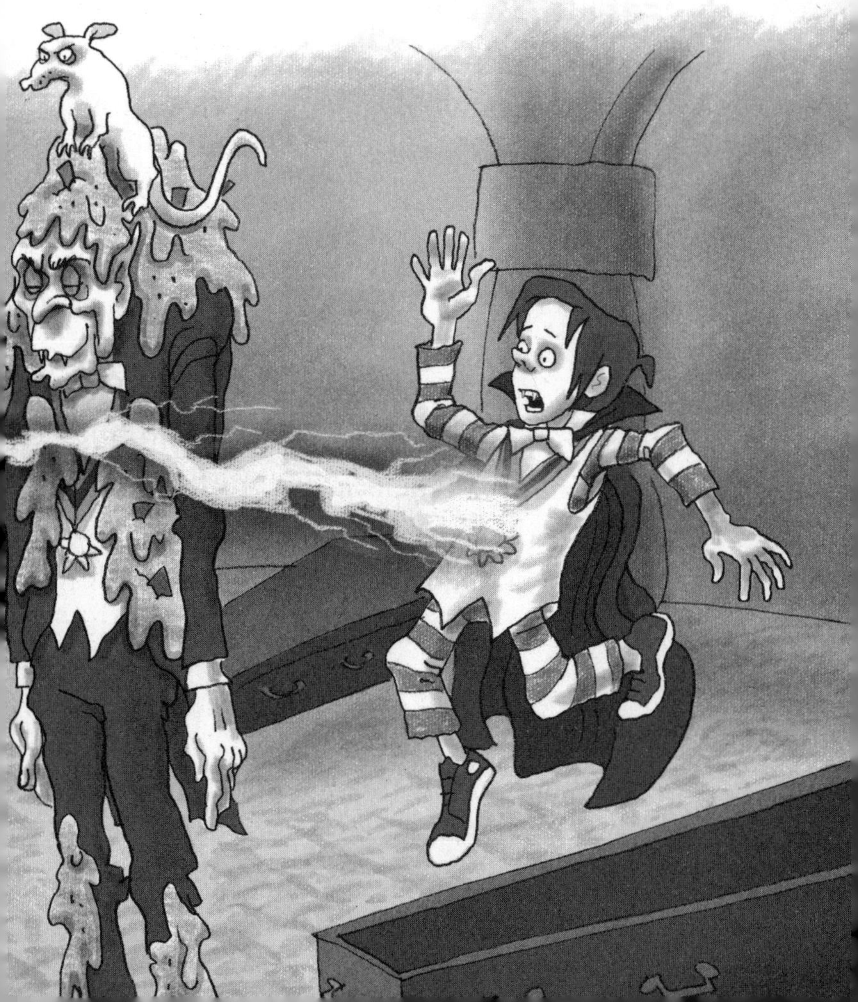

Cody tried to run away, but he couldn't move. The demon tapped Cody's forehead with his staff.

"Ow!"

Then he tapped Farley's zombie head. *Thwap.*

He tapped Rasputin's head.

"Squeak!"

Again and again he tapped everyone's heads. "Ow!" *Thwap.* "Squeak!" "Ow!" *Thwap.* "Squeak!" Cody was sure the demon was going to bust his skull right open.

Then, suddenly, the demon god of destruction raised both hands high and triumphant in the air. His staff brushed the cobwebs on the ceiling. He opened his mouth wide and roared. "Raaaaaaaagghhh!"

A booming, banging noise filled the crypt like a gunshot. Smoke flew everywhere. Cody fell flat on his back. Farley and Rasputin toppled onto him.

I'm dead, Cody thought. *I died pinned underneath a brain-dead vampire.*

Sully and the other boys ran over to Cody and lifted him up.

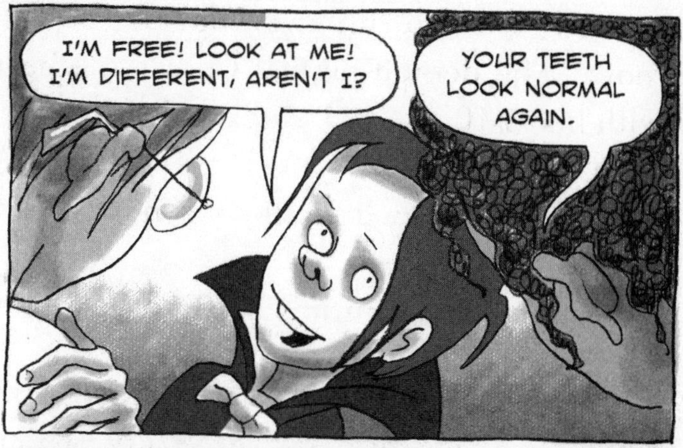
I'M FREE! LOOK AT ME! I'M DIFFERENT, AREN'T I?
YOUR TEETH LOOK NORMAL AGAIN.

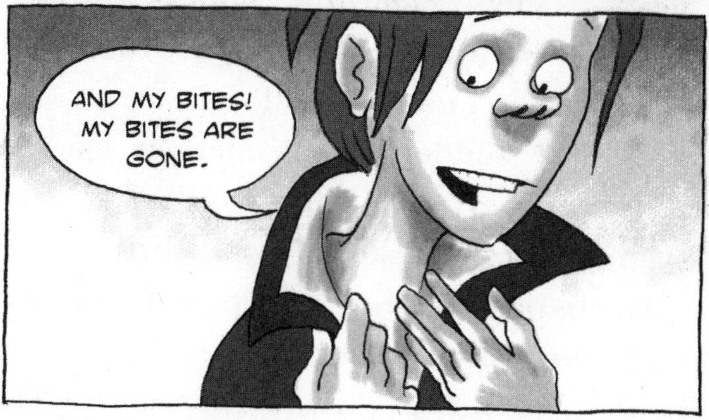
AND MY BITES! MY BITES ARE GONE.

"I'm better now," Cody said. "I can feel it. No more vampire stuff. I can just tell."

"But if you're better," Carlos said, "then what about . . ."

They all turned to look at Farley. He still lay on the ground, his limbs twitching. Then they went still. His eyes popped open.

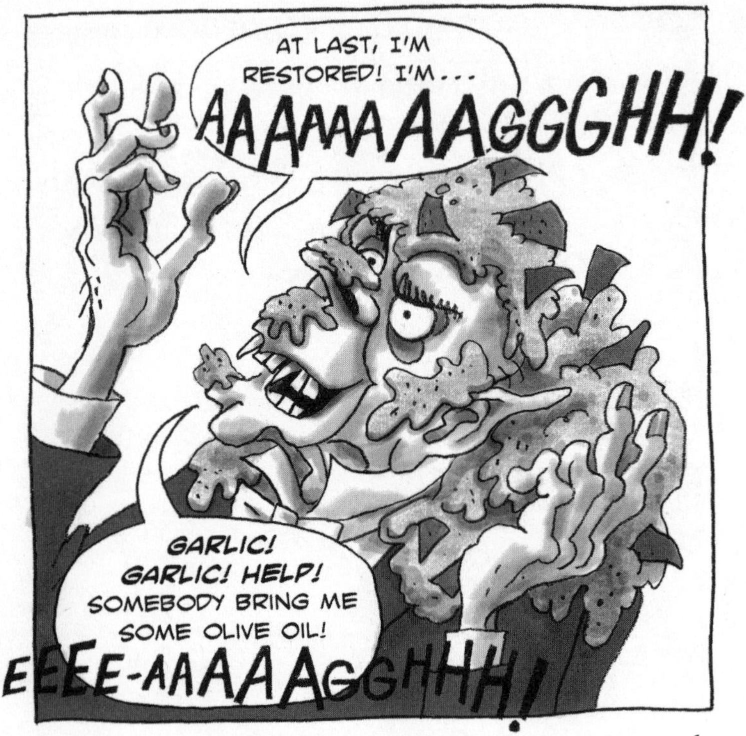
AT LAST, I'M RESTORED! I'M...
AAAAAAAAGGGHH!
GARLIC! GARLIC! HELP! SOMEBODY BRING ME SOME OLIVE OIL!
EEEE-AAAAAGGHHH!

He hopped, he shrieked, he screamed, but the more he rubbed at his eyes and face, the more he smeared the garlic around. He did a frenzied dance just trying to fling the garlic off himself. Bits of garlic powder and paste scattered all over the crypt.

"I have to say, I'll take garlic smell over dead body smell any day," Victor said.

"You saved me, guys," Cody said. "Thanks. I owe you, big-time, forever."

Farley wiped the garlic off his face and glared at the boys with oozing, bloodshot eyes.

"Save the speeches, Cody," Sully whispered. "Our 'forever' is probably only another three minutes, tops."

CHAPTER SIXTEEN

THE BEETLE

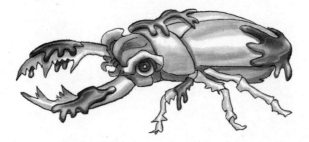

Farley dropped to his knees in front of the demon and raised his hands high.

"O great Ramut," he cried. "Mighty Destroyer, Devourer of Souls, I offer you the Beetle of Infinite Power. Grant me the Lizard of Endless Dominion over Children!"

The Beetle of Infinite Power?

Victor elbowed Sully. "When did lizards enter the picture?"

"Ssh!" Sully hissed. *"It's hanging from Ramut's neck!"*

Ramut pointed his scepter at Cody's beetle. Farley turned and smiled.

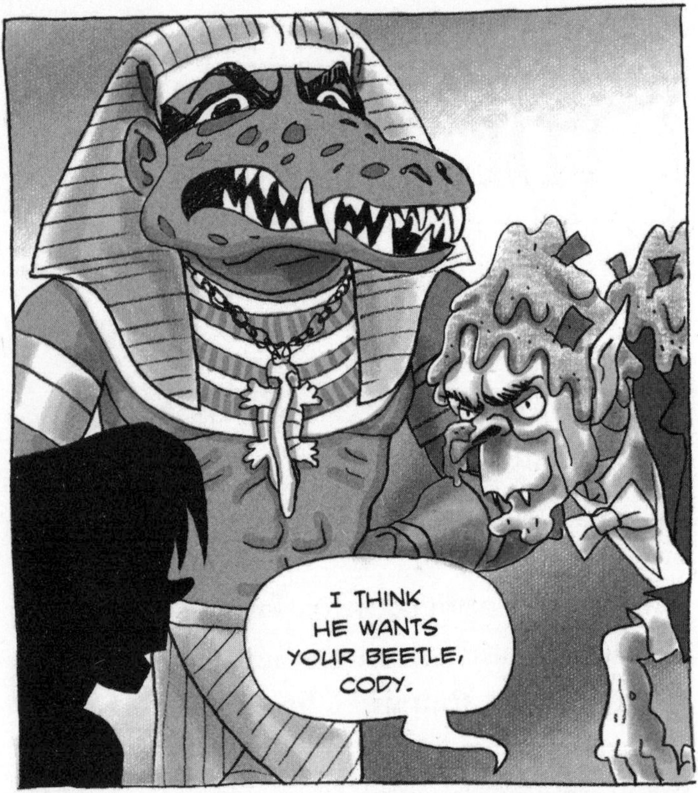
I THINK HE WANTS YOUR BEETLE, CODY.

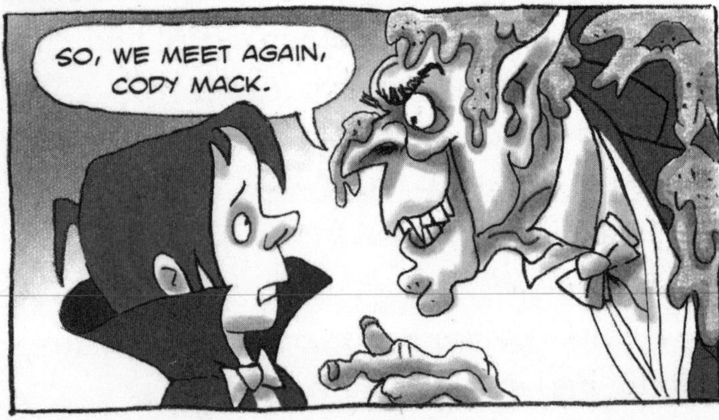
SO, WE MEET AGAIN, CODY MACK.

"You played a most helpful role in restoring me to my full powers. Remind me to thank you properly someday. But now, to business. Hand over the beetle."

"Hand over the *what*?" Cody said.

"You can't fool me, lad," Farley snapped. "I know where you wear it. I led you to it and showed you how to use it."

Whatever you do, don't give him the beetle, Cody thought.

"So, uh, where'd you find a Beetle of Infinite Power, anyway?" Cody said, edging half an inch toward the door. "Do they sell them at the mall?"

"Don't be stupid," Farley said. "Give it to me."

Cody ooched a little closer to the door. "You're right, that was stupid of me," he said. "They'd never let a creep like you in the mall."

The other boys followed Cody's lead. There was nothing they could do to stop Farley, not now that he had his full vampire powers. Cody knew that. But it felt better having his friends close by.

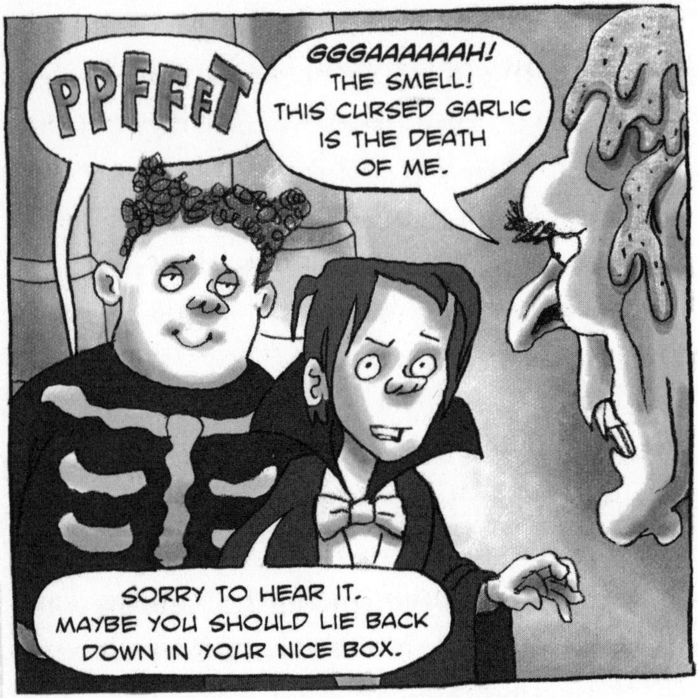
PPFFFT
GGGAAAAAAH!
THE SMELL!
THIS CURSED GARLIC
IS THE DEATH
OF ME.
SORRY TO HEAR IT.
MAYBE YOU SHOULD LIE BACK
DOWN IN YOUR NICE BOX.

"Give me the beetle, Cody Brat," Farley said, "or I shall be forced to make things very unpleasant for you."

"You never did tell me where you found him," Cody said. *Closer. Closer.*

"Egypt," Farley said. "Obviously."

Ramut still stood like a statue. Cody crept closer to the door. "When did you go to Egypt?"

"When I was a little boy," Farley said.

Closer. "If you've had a Beetle of Infinite Power, how come you never used it?"

"None of your beeswax," Farley snapped. He smoothed his tie but forgot he was a walking stalk of garlic glop. "The beetle was cursed. Anyone who took it from its true resting place would fail in his quest for power and lose the beetle."

Cody was halfway to the door now. "You mean to say," he said, "you had the beetle, and then you lost it, and it's been loose in your dungeons ever since?"

"*You* were able to keep it," Farley said, "because you didn't steal it. You cheated. That beetle only stayed with you because it liked you, though why anything would want to hang around near your repulsive neck is more than I can fathom. Every time I bit your neck as Rasputin, I had to gargle with salt water afterward. Little boys taste *vile*."

Cody took another step. He had reached the sarcophagus. He was almost to the door!

"We don't taste vile," Cody said, still edging closer. He was almost home free! "I mean, um, yeah. We sure do!"

Gggrrrowwwwwl.

Ramut pointed at Cody. In a flash, Farley realized it, too. Cody and the boys were almost to the door. Ramut flung his scepter toward the door. It clattered on the steps and transformed . . .

Into a giant, hooded cobra!

Shoot.

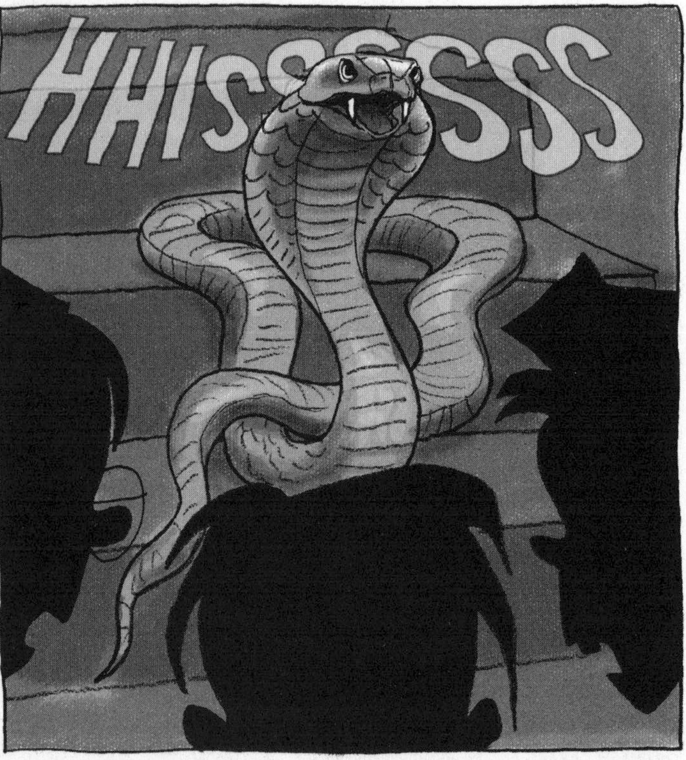
HHISSSSSS

Cody backed away, bumping into the sarcophagus.

"Give me the beetle, Cody Mack," Farley said, "and I promise you that your gruesome death will be swift."

Cody reached into his shirt for the beetle. Was he really going to give in to his archenemy? Never!

He pulled it away from his neck, and the golden bands dissolved. He held in his hands the living, stinking beetle with its constantly twitching, probing feelers and creepy-crawly legs. He didn't really have a plan for what he was going to do with it. But Farley made a grab for it, so Cody held it high over his head.

Brrrzzzz. Brrrzzzz.

Ramut opened his great jaws and roared. The blast from his angry breath nearly knocked Cody over.

Brrrzzzz. Brrrzzzz.

What could Cody do?

He opened his mouth to speak.

And suddenly, words appeared in his mind. So he yelled them for all he was worth.

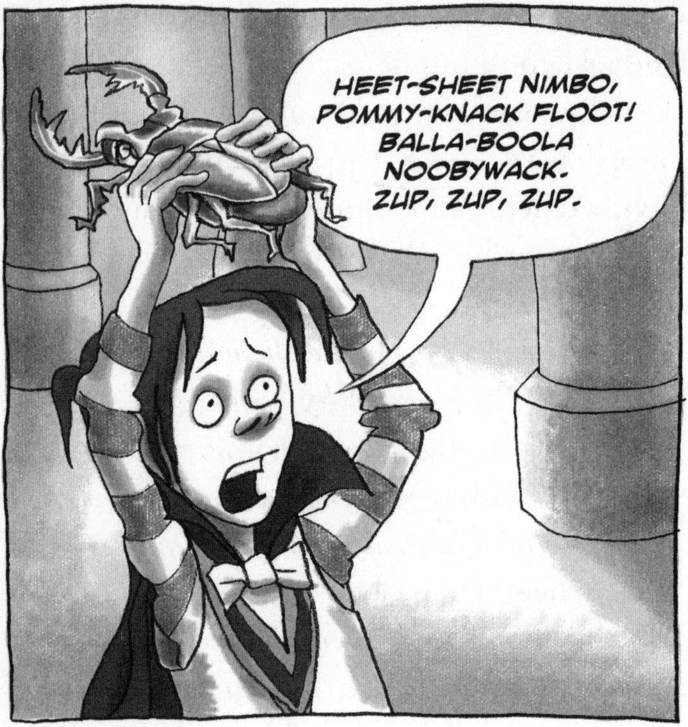
HEET-SHEET NIMBO, POMMY-KNACK FLOOT! BALLA-BOOLA NOOBYWACK. ZUP, ZUP, ZUP.

Ramut and Farley flapped their arms like chicken wings!

They looked at each other. Farley looked confused. Ramut looked—could it be?—afraid.

"Cody's cracked," Carlos said sadly. "De-vampiring him was more than his poor brain could take."

"What are you, blind?" Sully replied. To

Cody he called, "Whatever you're doing, Cody, keep doing it!"

Sully was right. Whatever Ramut and Farley were doing, they weren't eating the boys. At least not while Cody chanted his strange words. Where on earth were they coming from?

Let's see if I can make them do the Bunny Hop, Cody thought. *Why not?*

He spoke what came into his mind.

"Differ donder lulu, makka-moo flee,
Kizmo poofypie, my-a buy-a rumba."

The beetle was telling him what to say! At least, that's what it felt like. While Cody chanted, Ramut and Farley tried, and failed, to pat their heads while rubbing their bellies and spinning in a circle. With every strange syllable, Ramut's aura faded.

The beetle glowed. He was angry.

"Wow, this really *is* a Beetle of Infinite Power," Cody said. "I'm more powerful than a demon god *and* a vampire! I can bust us out of here, and destroy Splurch Academy, and send us home."

The other boys cheered.

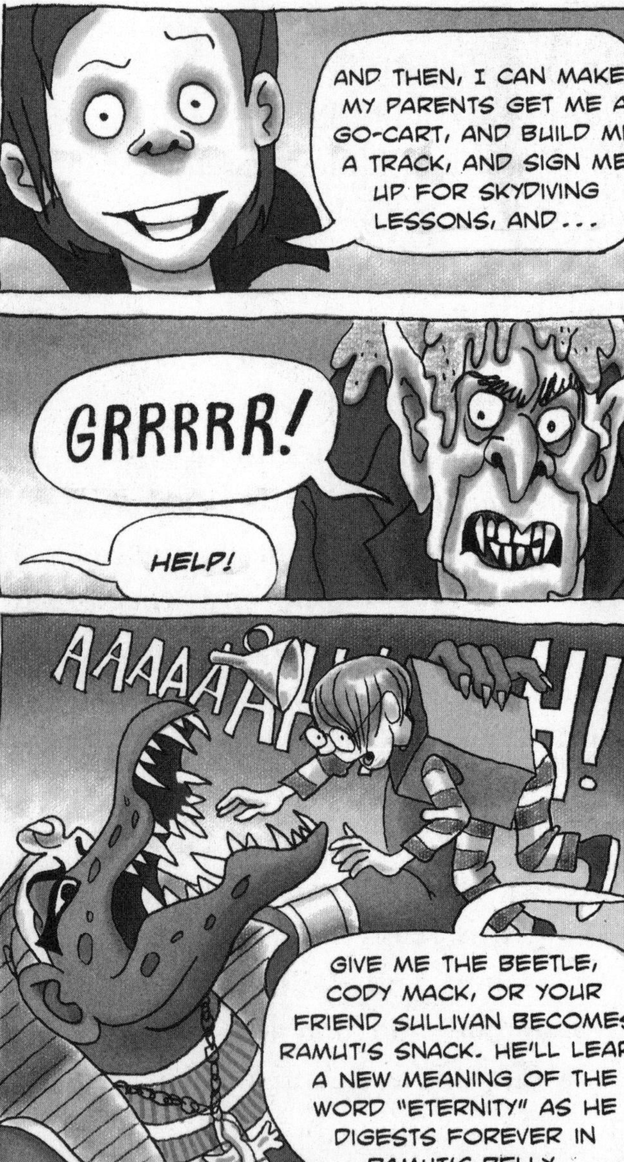
AND THEN, I CAN MAKE MY PARENTS GET ME A GO-CART, AND BUILD ME A TRACK, AND SIGN ME UP FOR SKYDIVING LESSONS, AND . . .
GRRRRRR!
HELP!
AAAAAAAAAAAH!
GIVE ME THE BEETLE, CODY MACK, OR YOUR FRIEND SULLIVAN BECOMES RAMUT'S SNACK. HE'LL LEARN A NEW MEANING OF THE WORD "ETERNITY" AS HE DIGESTS FOREVER IN RAMUT'S BELLY.

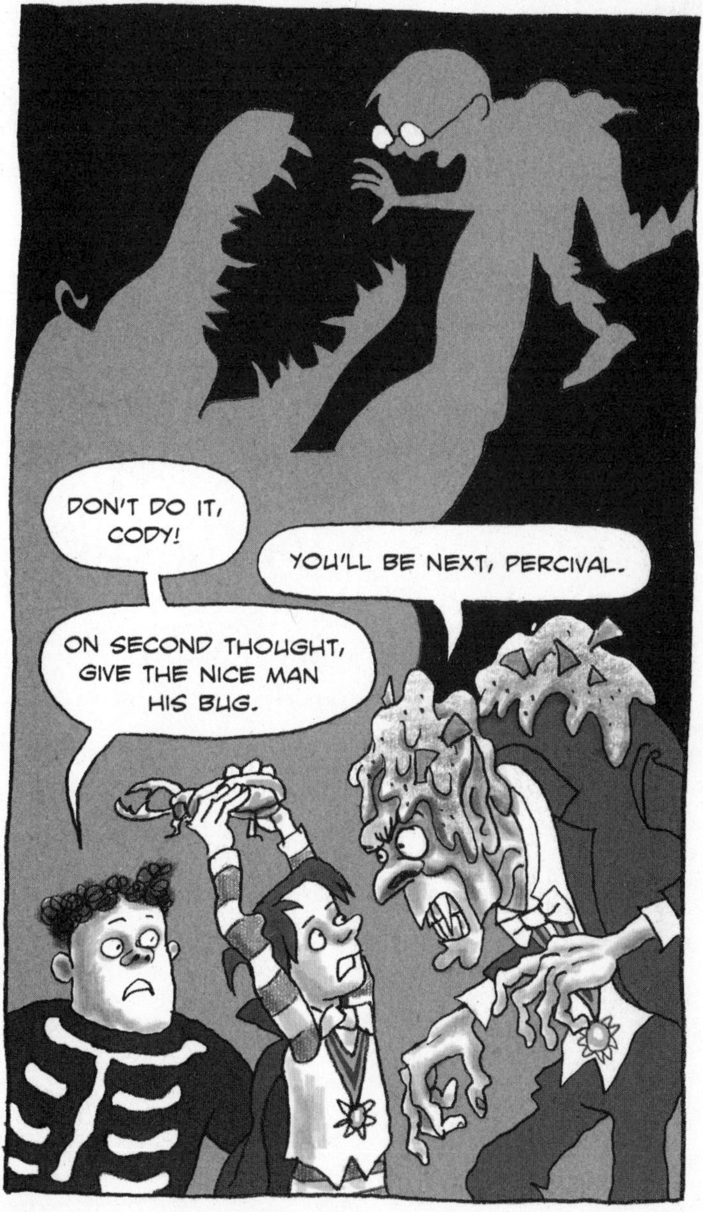
DON'T DO IT, CODY!
YOU'LL BE NEXT, PERCIVAL.
ON SECOND THOUGHT, GIVE THE NICE MAN HIS BUG.

Cody held the beetle even higher in the air. *C'mon, magic words,* he thought, *tell me what to say so I can save my friends and stop this demon-turkey once and for all.*

Ramut spun Sully over his wide open jaws.

Cody lowered the bug. He didn't have enough control over its magic to know for sure that he could save the others. He handed the hissing, squirting beetle to Archibald Farley.

"*Aaaaaaahhhh,*" Farley said. "At last! The Lizard will soon be mine!"

"Not so fast, you creep," Mugsy yelled, and he aimed a squirt of garlic paste in Farley's eye. But the garlic barely fazed the headmaster now. Both he and Ramut stopped in their tracks as the door to the sarcophagus slowly creaked open . . .

And the Splurch Academy librarian appeared.

CHAPTER SEVENTEEN

THE MUMMY

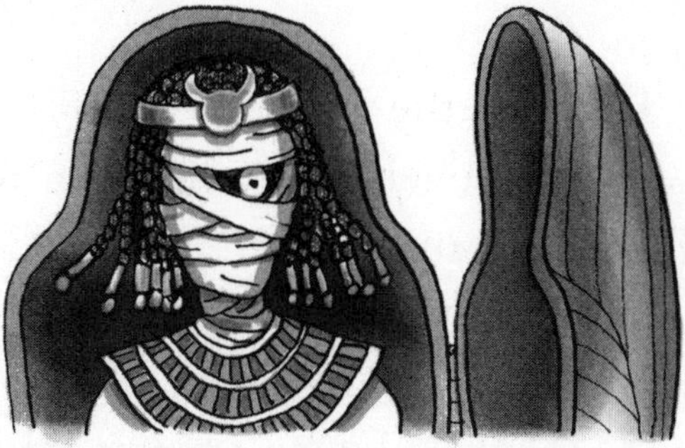

Her?

Out she came from her upright tomb. Ramut and Farley froze where they stood.

She didn't look like she usually did in the library. She was dressed differently, for one thing. A dry, angry sound rose from her throat to fill the gloomy crypt, and she held her arms high in a karate-chop formation.

Ramut and Farley's eyes bugged out of their heads.

"I'm seeing things, right, Cody?" Carlos whispered. "Tell me that's not our librarian. She shows up at the weirdest times."

Ramut made a loud, growly, whiny sound. It was like the terrified yelp of a mighty crocodile that's just gone completely chicken. The demon-god dropped Sully like yesterday's tissue. He fell to the ground with a thud.

The mummy librarian clapped her bandaged hands together, and Sully was lifted off the ground and dropped back down safely by the other boys.

Then her gaze fell upon Farley. The librarian hissed at him, and his knees began to tremble.

"Y-YOU?!" he stammered. "One of my own staff? You're the High Priestess-Queen Hatshepsut? *You're the lady pharaoh?*"

She didn't answer. She only hissed and pointed a menacing arm at Farley.

"But your mummy was never found! You . . . you can't exist!"

The mummy's gaze fell on the beetle Farley clutched in his hands.

She let out a cry of joy, and held out both her arms.

The beetle buzzed, straining to reach her.

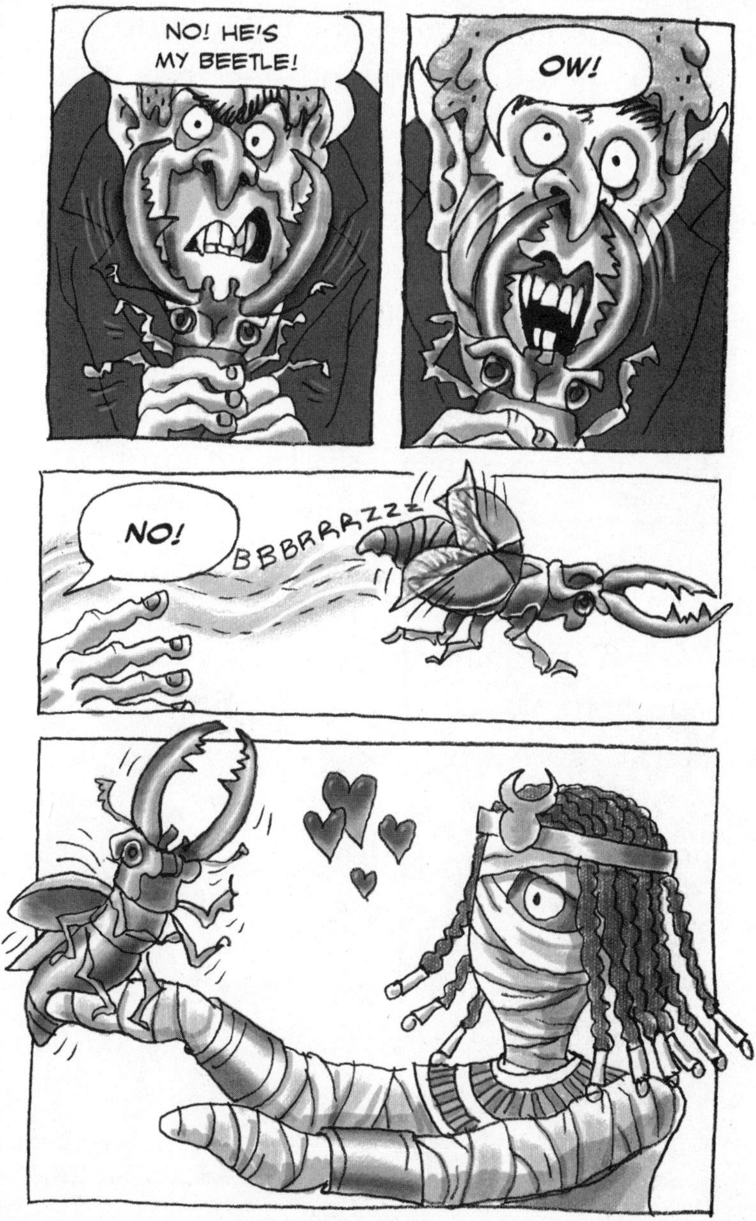
NO! HE'S MY BEETLE!
OW!
NO!
BBBRRRRZZZ

Ramut the Destroyer bolted for the exit. He grabbed his cobra and it turned back into a scepter.

"Wait, stop!" Farley cried. "My Lizard of Endless Dominion Over Children!"

But Ramut was deaf to Farley's pleas. He blasted up the stairs, lizard and all.

"Stinks to be Farley," Carlos whispered.

"Pee-yew," Ratface said. "You can say that again. He's the Garlic Death Lord."

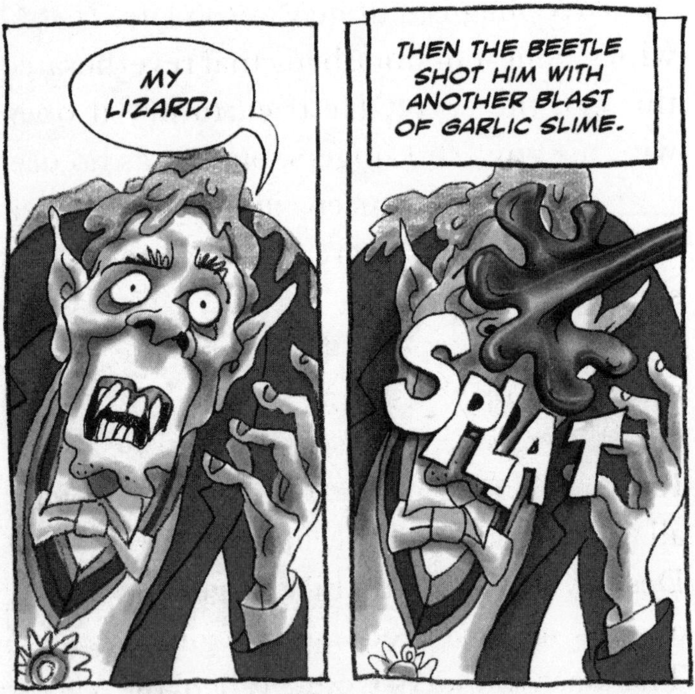
MY LIZARD!
THEN THE BEETLE SHOT HIM WITH ANOTHER BLAST OF GARLIC SLIME.
SPLAT

The Splurch mummy librarian, or Pharaoh-Queen Hatshepsut, whoever she was, turned and walked stiffly back to her opened sarcophagus. She backed inside it, still cradling her beetle. It clasped its pincers around her neck, and the mummy made a windy, wispy sighing sound. The heavy sarcophagus door slowly closed.

"Noooo!" Farley cried. "At least I can still have the beetle!" He scrambled over to the sarcophagus, but he was too late. It shut with a stone-on-stone bang that reverberated through the crypt. He tried to pry it open with his powerful fingers, but it was no use.

The pharaoh-queen and her beloved beetle were back where they belonged, and staying there.

"C'mon, let's go." Cody and the others scrambled up the stairs.

They reached the surface in time to see Ramut plow through the partygoers, who all fell back, whimpering in terror. The Destroyer snapped his fingers. A bolt of lightning snaked down from the sky. The flash blinded Cody. When his vision returned, the demon was gone, leaving a circle of charred grass.

"Run!" Cody said. The boys hitched up their costumes and sprinted across the lawn before the dazed monsters could regain their senses.

"What happened down there?" a monster voice said. "If it scared *that* dude, I don't want to wait around to meet it." Monsters took off flying, slithering, and waddling, scattering like marbles.

The boys reached the door and heaved it open. Safe, inside. They slid down onto the floor and collapsed. Who'd have thought they'd ever be so happy to be back inside Splurch Academy?

CHAPTER EIGHTEEN

THE END?

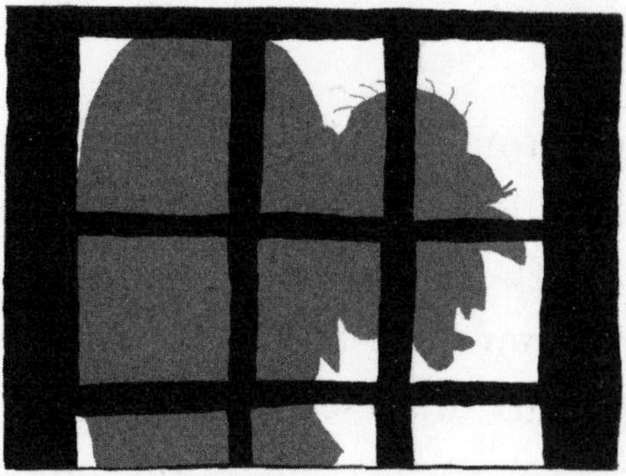

"Back in the dorms," Ratface observed as they crawled into bed that night. "I guess quarantine is over."

"Yeah," Carlos said. "We've had a miracle cure from our . . . what was it? Gagged Splaskers?"

"Splagged gaskers," Sully said. "Close enough."

"Where've you clowns been?" asked an older boy from one of the other grades. "We figured you'd been eaten."

"We got to go on a special field trip," Victor said.

"Just so long as you didn't bring Farley back with you," the older kid joked. "Splurch Academy's been way better since he's been gone."

Cody and his friends looked at one another.

"The words *Splurch Academy* and *way better* don't even belong in the same sentence," Carlos said.

"Sure they do," Victor said. "It'd be *way better* to die the death of a thousand paper cuts than to ever be sent to Splurch Academy."

"Which is better? To torch Splurch Academy, or use a wrecker ball? Demolishing Splurch Academy with ten thousand sticks of dynamite would be *way better*," Sully said.

"The food at Splurch Academy is bad, but at least with lots of ketchup it's *way better*," Mugsy added.

"Never mind," the older kid said, rolling over in his bunk. "Forget I said anything at all, okay? And let the rest of us get some sleep."

The door to the dormitory opened. There, in the glow from the hallway candles, stood a tall, familiar figure with a rat perched on his shoulder.

The older kid let out a shocked breath. "Rats! It's him!"

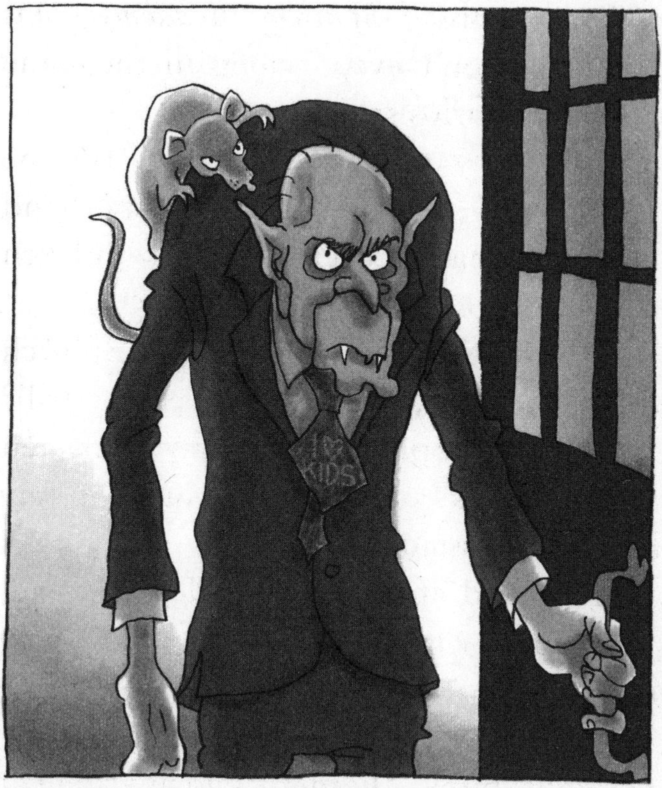
KIDS

It was him, all right. Archibald Farley, Headmaster of Splurch Academy, was back from the grave and boiling mad at Cody and his friends. He couldn't bite them, not now that he had his body back and had to abide by the ancient rules governing the Academy —rules ensuring that, so long as the children didn't go outside after dark, the monsters could never eat them. He wouldn't risk breaking them again, not directly. But he could still find all sorts of ways to make their lives a living misery.

And Cody knew he was the first kid Farley would start with, any time he wanted to test out some new torture method.

SWEET DREAMS. YOU BOYS HAVE NO IDEA HOW I'VE MISSED YOU. BUT YOU'LL FIND OUT TOMORROW.

He pulled the door shut.

"We're all goners," Cody moaned.

"Look at the bright side, Cody," Carlos whispered. "You're yourself again. No more vampire mind-control. We won that part."

"But we brought Farley back," Cody said.

"We stopped him from getting a Lizard of Endless Dominion over Children," Sully pointed out. "That's something."

"What difference does it make?" Cody said. "He's got endless dominion over us."

"Will you quit blabbing about lizards?" the older kid grunted. "I'm trying to sleep."

Cody stared into the darkness.

"Hey, guys." It was Mugsy, whispering. "Guys. Follow me. Come see what I got."

Mugsy led them into the bathroom.

"When we were passing through the party," Mugsy said, "I, er, grabbed a few things." He poured out a pillowcase onto the tile floor. Inside were pounds and pounds of confiscated Halloween candy and treats.

"There may be a few bugs mixed in, but who cares?" he said. "Happy Halloween, guys."

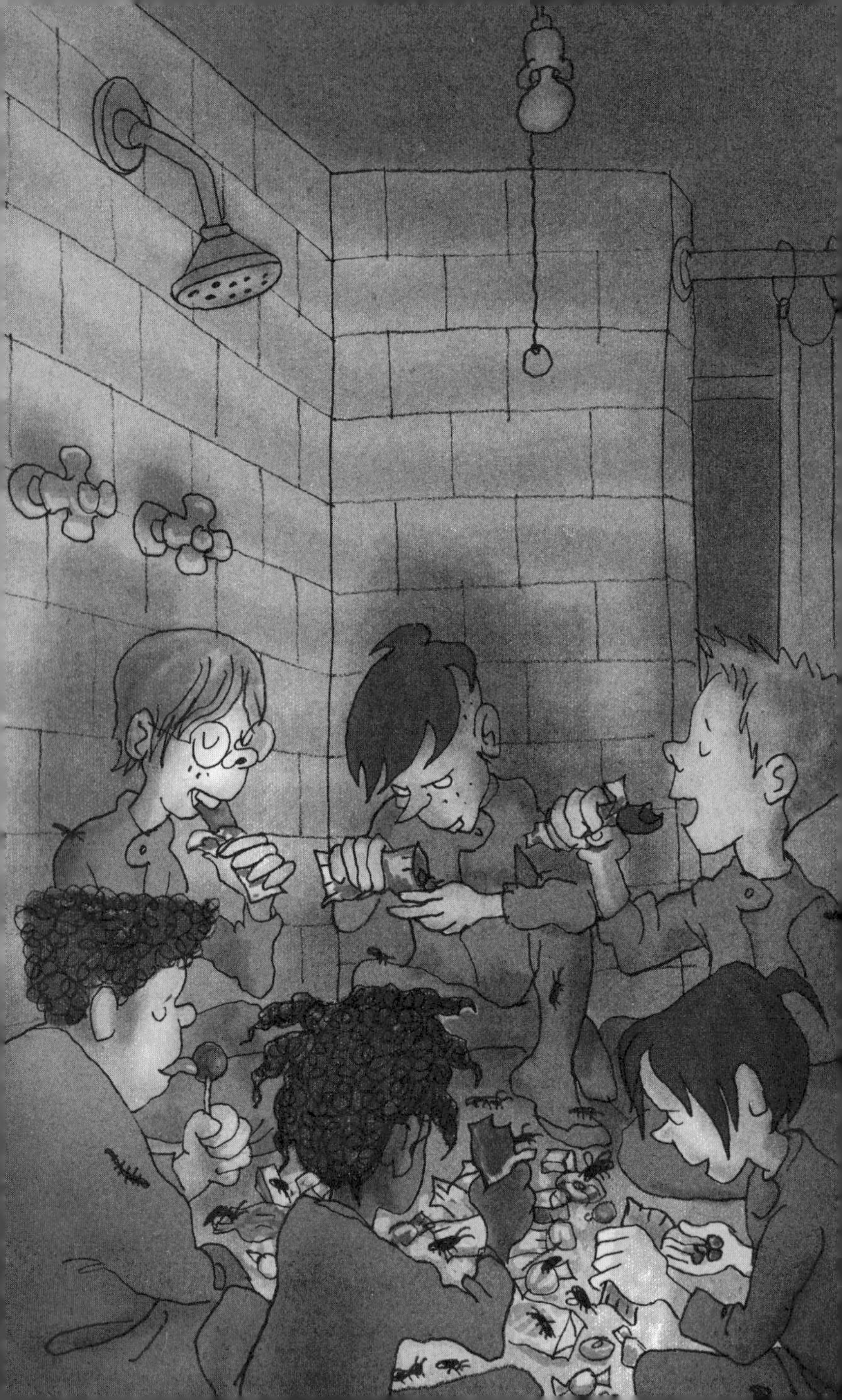

Acknowledgments

Special thanks to our sister,
Joanna Gardner, for tirelessly Splurching
along with us. There's a room with a view
in Splurch's topmost tower with her name
on it. Thanks also to our mom, Shirley
Gardner, for all the bowls of oatmeal.

About the Authors

Sally Faye Gardner and Julie Gardner Berry are sisters, both originally from upstate New York. Sally, who now lives in New York City with a smallish black dog named Dottie, has, at various times, worked as a gas pumper, janitor, sign painter, meeting attendee, and e-mail sender. Julie, who now lives near Boston with her husband, four smallish sons, and tiger cat named Coco, has worked as a restaurant busboy, volleyball referee, cleaning lady, and seller of tight leather pants. Today she, too, attends meetings and sends e-mail. Julie is the author of *The Amaranth Enchantment* and *Secondhand Charm*, while this is Sally's first series.